HEARTSCAPES

What Reviewers Say About MJ Williamz's Work

Visit us at www.boldstrokesbooks.com

By the Author

Shots Fired

Forbidden Passions

Initiation by Desire

Speakeasy

Escapades

Sheltered Love

Summer Passion

Heartscapes

HEARTSCAPES

by

MJ Williamz

2016

ISBN 13: 978-1-62639-532-9

This Trade Paperback Original Is Published By
Bold Strokes Books, Inc.
P.O. Box 249
Valley Falls, NY 12185

First Edition: April 2016

CREDITS
Editor: Cindy Cresap
Production Design: Susan Ramundo
Cover Design By Sheri (graphicartist2020@hotmail.com)

Acknowledgments

First and foremost, I want to thank Laydin, without whom none of this would be possible. There are several other people to thank in the making of this book—Shawn Marie for her help with Art School information and Laura Sisco for her help with French. I'd also like to thank Sarah and Dawn for reading over the book for me. And, as always, thanks for Rad for publishing me and to Cindy for working with me to make this book what it is.

Dedication

To Laydin—For everything

CHAPTER ONE

Jesse Garrett ran her hand over the empty bed next to her. Cold. The woman from the night before was obviously long gone. She remembered the talented tongue and nimble fingers, but like everything else good in her life, it was all just a memory now.

She lay back and stared at her ceiling, the familiar sense of emptiness washing over her. She knew she had to get ready to meet Liza for lunch, but she wasn't in any hurry. She had plenty of time. As she lay there, memories of happier times came to her and made her want to cry. Rather than dwell in the past, she got out of bed and took her shower.

The hot water pelted her skin and wakened her senses. It felt good to wash away the woman from the previous night and their sex. She needed to be clean, fresh, and ready for the new day.

Jesse arrived at Mama Serrano's in the Museum District of Houston shortly before one o'clock. She was always early, but Liza apparently had anticipated this, as Jesse saw her car in the parking lot and pulled in next to her.

Liza rose and greeted Jesse with a hug. Jesse looked at her best friend of twenty years and marveled again at how different they were. Liza was tall, blond, and thin. And very feminine. All things Jesse was not.

"Did you have a good time last night?" Liza asked.

"Yep."

"Good. You and Mandy really seemed to hit it off."

"Was that her name?" Jesse said.

Liza rolled her eyes.

"Yes, that was her name. Did you two have a nice morning? Breakfast in bed and all that?"

"No. She was gone when I woke up."

"Honestly, Jesse. How do you do that?"

"What? Make them leave? Just lucky I guess."

"Don't you get tired of that?"

"Not at all. Why would I?"

"I worry about you."

"I don't. You shouldn't either," Jesse said. She looked up at the painting of the dessert on the wall. "That's really a beautiful work of art."

"Don't change the subject, young lady."

"Young lady? At thirty-nine, I thank you very much for that moniker."

"Seriously, Jesse. When are all these nameless encounters going to end?"

"When I'm too old for those young ladies to want to come home with me."

"Mandy was a sweetheart. She was totally into you. You had a lot in common. How could you have scared her away? Last night at the dance, she would have followed you to the moon."

"Maybe because I told her I didn't want more than a night."

"How are you ever going to move on if you won't be with a woman for more than a night?"

Jesse's eyes misted over. It had been four years, yet the thought of moving on still made her cry.

"I'm sorry, Jess."

"I'm not ready, Liza."

"I know. And I'm sorry I push you. But I just think all these one-night stands can't be good for you."

"Liza, those one-night stands are what keep me going. I'm numb all day every day. The only time I feel anything, anything at all, is when I'm in bed with a woman. Then, and only then, do I feel alive. But I don't want more than that brief moment, because anything else would be untrue to Sara's memory."

"And you think sleeping with every woman in town is being true to her?"

"I don't think she would begrudge me the most basic of human needs."

Liza laughed.

"Some people think food, water, and shelter are basic needs," she said.

"So is the touch of another. And good sex is my favorite kind of touch."

"You need to find something to do that interests you. I mean really interests you. You're in a dead-end job, you have no hobbies, you wallow away in grief. You need to find something to live for, Jesse."

Jesse considered Liza's words. She knew she was right about the dead-end job. She worked for an insurance company, and there was no future in it for her. She just went to work every day, did her monotonous job, and came home. There was no challenge, no burning desire to do more or learn more or take on more responsibilities. But there never had been. Even before Sara's death, she'd been simply going through the motions at work.

"What about your art?" Liza asked.

"That was something I did a long time ago. I was never any good at it, and I'm not interested in it anymore."

"You were really good at it."

"That's very kind of you to say, but I wasn't. It was just something to do."

"Well, you need something to do now," Liza said.

"No. I don't. Not that, anyway. I have my job. I have the dances every other week. I have you. I don't need a hobby."

"I think you need something to keep your hands and mind busy."

"I appreciate your concern, but I'm fine, Liza."

"I think you've mourned long enough, Jesse."

"I will never have mourned long enough, Liza. Never."

❖

The Houston Womyn's Society held dances every other Saturday night in different venues around the city. Jesse was excited to attend that week's at The Black Hole. It was one of her favorite lesbian clubs. She took her time getting ready for it, showering slowly, letting the water caress her like she was sure a lover would later that night. She dressed in black jeans and a dark purple golf shirt that accentuated her eyes. A little gel in her hair and she was ready for Liza to pick her up. She sat down and opened a beer to wait.

Liza and Jesse arrived at The Black Hole a few minutes after nine, and the place was already filling up. The dances started at eight thirty, as they tended to cater to older lesbians. But there were always plenty of younger women there, too, out to dance and have a good time. Jesse didn't consider herself to be a cougar, but younger women seemed to find her attractive, and she wasn't about to complain. Of course, she knew she didn't look her age, which helped.

She made her way to the bar and bought drinks for herself and Liza. They had a table just on the edge of the dance floor, a perfect spot to see and be seen. The music and women made Jesse's constant state of numbness disappear. She felt alive and vibrant. She was bouncing her foot and bobbing her head in time to the music when a woman walked up to her.

"Are you two together?" the woman whispered in her ear.

Jesse shook her head.

"Then would you like to dance?"

"Sure."

The woman had shoulder length auburn hair and light green eyes. She had freckles across the bridge of her nose, something Jesse found adorable, and unusual, as the woman was clearly in her late thirties or early forties.

They danced to a song from the eighties then left the dance floor, each walking to her own table.

"She was cute," Liza said.

"Yep." Jesse took a long pull from her beer. She scanned the room and turned back to see a young butch escorting Liza to the dance floor. The woman was wearing sagging, baggy cargo pants and a shirt at least two sizes too big. Jesse was thankful that hadn't been the style when she was a baby butch.

She searched the crowd, and her gaze landed on an attractive woman two tables over. She was probably in her thirties, with long blond hair and curves that made Jesse's mouth water. She put on her most confident stride as she approached the woman.

"Would you like to dance?" she asked.

"Sure."

They moved to the beat, and Jesse loved the way the woman's breasts bounced to the rhythm of the music. She could watch her all night. The song ended and a slow song started. Jesse thought it would be wonderful to feel the woman's body pressed to her.

"What do you say?" she asked.

"No, thanks," the woman answered, walking away and leaving Jesse standing on the dance floor.

Jesse walked back to her table to find baby butch still chatting up Liza. She arched her eyebrows at Liza who just smiled.

When the slow song ended, another woman asked Jesse to dance. She ended up dancing most of the night, but not connecting with anyone. She really wanted a chance with the blonde and finally worked her way back over to her table.

"Would you like to dance again?"

"You're persistent, aren't you?"

"Actually, I'm Jesse," Jesse joked. She extended a hand. "It's nice to meet you."

The woman laughed.

"I'm Chanelle."

"I like that name."

"Thank you."

"So, about that dance?"

"Sure. Why not?"

They danced three more songs, talking to each other as best they could over the music as they moved.

The beat slowed down again and Jesse looked at Chanelle.

"What do you say?"

"Sure. Why not?"

Chanelle moved into Jesse's arms and Jesse held her loosely, cautious not to pull her as close as she'd like. She was enjoying the tease of Chanelle's breasts against her and wanted to feel them fully pressed into her. Later, she told herself, certain she'd be able to lure Chanelle back to her place.

The dance ended, and Jesse reached for Chanelle's hand. Chanelle stopped in her tracks and looked at Jesse.

"Too much?" Jesse asked. "I really like you."

"What does that mean? I mean, I like you, too, but I'm not in the market for a girlfriend right now."

"Neither am I."

"Well, you sure seem possessive."

"I apologize," Jesse said. "I'd just like to have you with me tonight."

"That's doable."

They walked back to Jesse's table and Jesse signaled the waitress for two more drinks. Liza was out on the dance floor, making out with the same young butch. Jesse had to laugh at them. But she was happy they'd both get lucky that night.

She and Chanelle talked about lots of things as they enjoyed several drinks. She was really enjoying Chanelle's company.

Another slow song started, and Jesse led Chanelle to the floor. She wrapped her arms around Chanelle and held her close, relishing the feel of her curves against her. She tilted Chanelle's face up and looked into her eyes. She saw a longing that matched her own.

Jesse kept her gaze locked on Chanelle's as she lowered her head. She saw Chanelle's full lips part just before she closed her eyes. Their first kiss was soft and slow, leaving Jesse wanting more. She pulled back, but met resistance as Chanelle drew her head back down.

This time, Chanelle opened her mouth and welcomed Jesse's tongue. Jesse let her tongue enter slowly, tentatively, at first and felt her heart race when it met Chanelle's. She pulled Chanelle closer to her, cupping her ass as she did. The feel of the soft flesh spurred her on, and she moved her tongue deeper into Chanelle's mouth, claiming every inch of it.

The song ended and they were still kissing. Chanelle finally pulled away, breaking the kiss.

"That was something," Jesse said, breathless.

"Yeah, it was."

"You want to dance some more?"

"I think I'd rather take this back to my place."

"Actually, I didn't drive, so if you have a car, let's just go back to my place."

"Oh, yeah. Otherwise I'd just have to give you a ride in the morning and that would be awkward. Come on. Let's go."

Jesse was so happy to have found a woman who understood her. There was a spring in her step as they left the bar.

Jesse fought the urge to molest Chanelle in the car on the way home. She couldn't wait to race her hands over those curves and feel the full extent of Chanelle's sensuality. They arrived at her house, and as soon as the front door was closed, were in each other's arms. Their kisses were passionate, their hands roaming freely over each other's bodies.

Jesse unbuttoned Chanelle's blouse and gasped at the size of her breasts, held firmly in place by a pink lacy bra.

"Dear God, you're beautiful," she breathed.

She helped Chanelle get her shirt off and pulled her own over her head. Jesse didn't wear a bra. She had small enough breasts that an undershirt worked for her. Chanelle pulled Jesse's undershirt off and cupped her breasts.

"These are nice," she said. She bent to kiss one nipple then the other.

Jesse felt her nipples pucker at the touch. She wanted to do the same to Chanelle and couldn't wait to get her breasts free of the confines of her bra. She reached around and deftly unhooked Chanelle's bra, watching her ample breasts fall free. She reached down and teased her nipples while Chanelle continued sucking hers.

She needed more, though. She needed to bury her face between them and suck the soft flesh. She wanted to suck on her nipples and feel them swell in her mouth. She wanted more than simply playing with them while standing.

"Let's get to bed," Jesse said.

She led the way down the hall and lay on her back while Chanelle straddled her, playing with her own tits. She fondled them, pressing them together, making Jesse squirm. When she sucked her own nipples, Jesse could take no more.

"You're killing me. Come here." She pulled Chanelle down so her breasts dangled just above her face. She sucked each nipple in turn, alternating licking them and taking them deep into her mouth. She wrapped both hands around one breast and suckled like her life depended on it. She couldn't remember the last time she'd enjoyed breasts so much.

Jesse reached one hand between Chanelle's legs and pressed the damp seam of her crotch into her.

Chanelle groaned.

"Oh God, that feels good."

"Mmhm," Jesse managed, still sucking away. She could stay like that forever, but the wetness she could feel through Chanelle's pants had her own jeans drenched. She finally released her oral grip.

"We need to get naked," she said.

Chanelle climbed off her and quickly stripped out of the rest of her clothes. Jesse did the same. Jesse pulled Chanelle to her in a passionate kiss. The feel of skin on skin made her dizzy with need. She ran her hands over Chanelle's back and ass and loved the soft, silky feel under her palms.

"Are you going to take me to bed or just stand here kissing me?" Chanelle finally said.

Jesse laughed.

"You'd better believe I'm taking you to bed."

They lay down facing each other.

"Do you have any idea how beautiful you are?" Jesse asked. "I mean, really?"

"You sure are a sweet talker."

"It's true. I want to take my time with you because your body is so hot. I want to enjoy every inch of it."

Chanelle rolled onto her back.

"Help yourself."

Jesse looked at the smorgasbord in front of her and didn't know where to start. She kissed Chanelle again. There was something about her kisses. They were soft yet passionate at the same time. She was a great kisser and Jesse was thoroughly enjoying her lips.

As they kissed, Jesse ran her hand down her chest and kneaded a breast. She closed her hand around it, ran her hand under it and over it, and finally took the nipple between her fingers. She pinched it and was rewarded when Chanelle moaned into her mouth. She twisted the nipple, pulling it harder, and Chanelle broke the kiss and threw her head back.

"Oh, yes. Oh God, yes."

Jesse moved her mouth to the nipple and sucked on it while she slid her hand lower over Chanelle's voluptuous body. She rubbed her belly, then slipped her hand between her open legs. She found her drenched and reveled in the feeling of her moisture all over her hand.

Chanelle moved under Jesse, encouraging her to explore more. Jesse massaged her swollen clit and was greeted with a guttural cry as Chanelle climaxed.

"That was easy," Jesse said.

"I guess I forgot to tell you how easy I am."

"No worries. Let's see what else we can do."

She buried her fingers deep inside Chanelle, and stroked her satin walls. Chanelle arched her back to take her deeper and Jesse plunged her fingers as deep as they would go. Chanelle cried out again as she reached her orgasm.

Jesse still wanted more. She couldn't get enough of Chanelle. She kissed down her stomach and finally positioned herself between her legs. The scent of Chanelle drove her wild. She lapped at all her juices and savored the flavor of her orgasms. Just the feel of her tongue seemed to be enough as Chanelle came again almost immediately.

Jesse didn't stop, though. She dipped her tongue inside her, licking every inch she could, then moved back to her clit, which she sucked and flicked. Chanelle pressed her face into her as she screamed out Jesse's name.

"No more," Chanelle said. "It's my turn now."

"But I'm not through," Jesse said. "You're delicious. I want to stay here."

"I can't take any more."

"Seriously?"

"Seriously."

Jesse climbed up next to Chanelle and kissed her, sharing her flavor with her.

"Tell me what you like," Chanelle said.

Jesse was taken aback at the question. She'd never thought to ask anyone that. She just did what felt good and what seemed to make her partner feel good.

"I want you to fuck me," Jesse said. "That's what I want."

"That I can do," Chanelle said. She sucked on Jesse's nipples as she slid her hand between her legs. Jesse was drenched after pleasing her and Chanelle commented on that.

"Someone's been having fun."

"You think?" Jesse was breathless with need. She wanted Chanelle to take her and take her fast. She needed to feel her inside and soon. She didn't want to wait any longer.

Chanelle wasted no more time. She slipped her fingers deep inside Jesse. She pulled them out slowly, then moved them back in. Over and over, she repeated this, with Jesse writhing on the bed, inching closer and closer to the climax she so craved.

"Oh God, you feel good," Jesse said.

"Yeah? You like this? You want more?"

"Oh yes, please."

Chanelle continued to move in and out of Jesse, pressing harder and deeper with each thrust. Jesse felt like her clit would burst, it was so swollen with desire.

"Rub my clit," she begged her.

"Not yet," Chanelle said.

Jesse was tempted to rub it herself, but gripped the sheets to keep from doing so. She was so close to an orgasm, but needed Chanelle to be the one to give it to her.

"Seriously. One touch and I'll come."

"I'm not ready for you to come yet."

For whatever reason, this turned Jesse on even more. She liked how take-charge Chanelle was. Chanelle moved around until her pussy was just over Jesse's mouth.

"Eat me again," she said, still working her fingers inside Jesse.

Jesse did, and Chanelle's orgasm ran down her face.

Chanelle blew on Jesse's clit. The feeling of the cool against her heated skin made Jesse shiver.

"Dear God, please, let me come."

Chanelle took her hand out of Jesse and traced circles around her swollen clit.

"Touch it. Please, touch it."

"When I'm ready."

Jesse's head was throbbing; she needed release so desperately.

Chanelle rubbed the underside of Jesse's clit, slowly moving her fingers up until she pressed directly on the sensitive nerve center.

Jesse screamed as she came, experiencing one of the most intense orgasms she'd ever had.

"You're cruel," Jesse said when Chanelle moved into her arms.

"But it was worth it, wasn't it?"

"It most certainly was."

"You're pretty good in bed," Chanelle said.

"Thanks. So are you."

"Too bad I'm not looking for more than a one-night stand."

"It's all good. Maybe we can hook up again some time," Jesse said, knowing she wouldn't do that. No matter how much fun they'd had, she would never take the same woman home twice.

CHAPTER TWO

L iza came over to Jesse's house the following day. She found Jesse in her pajamas, sitting in front of a television that wasn't even turned on.

"Whatcha doing?" Liza asked.

"Nothing."

"So I see."

"How was your night with the young one?"

"Her name is Clancy, and it was fun."

"Clancy? Sounds like a clown."

"At least I remember her name. And I'll see her again."

"Oh, so now you've met your soul mate?"

"Aren't you a bitch today? What's your problem?"

"Nothing. Sorry."

"How was your night?" Liza said.

"Fun."

"Good. She seemed nice enough."

"She was. And she was great in bed. And didn't want anything more. She was a dream."

"Sounds like you met your soul mate."

Jesse laughed.

"Sounds like I did."

"Well, there's a laugh anyway. I was worried about you. Mind if I sit down?"

"Not at all. And sorry. It's just a bad day today."

"I'm sorry, Jess."

"I miss her."

"I know you do. A nice romp usually helps your mood, though. I really wish we could find something to keep your mind occupied."

"Me, too, but I don't, so there you go."

"So I ask you again, what about your art?"

"I don't know."

"When was the last time you were in your studio?" Liza said.

"I haven't been out there since before Sara died."

"Let's go out there now. I want to see what you had going before you stopped."

"But Sara was my inspiration. I have none now."

"Well, you need to try." She reached her hand to Jesse. "Come on."

Jesse let her breath out and took Liza's hand. She didn't want to go out to her studio but knew Liza wouldn't let it go until they went. So she stood and steeled herself to go.

They crossed the backyard to a small outbuilding and Liza opened the door. Jesse smelled the paints and supplies and was instantly taken back to happier times when she'd lose herself in her work and Sara would bring her a cup of coffee and sit and watch her work. It was all about Sara. Sara's beauty was what made her paint. She'd sketched more pictures of Sara than anything else. Why bother now?

Liza stepped back to let Jesse step in first. Jesse's eyes watered and she wiped away the unshed tears. She took in the covered easels and half-finished art. She turned back to the door.

"I can't."

"Please, Jesse. Please try."

"I can't."

Liza pulled Jesse to her for a hug.

"It hurts so bad, Liza."

"Okay. Okay. I'm sorry. I just thought it would help."

Jesse pulled away and looked at the started sketches and half-finished paintings. Could she ever find it within herself to work on them again?

"Is there any pull? Any drive? Any desire?" Liza asked.

Jesse walked over and pulled the tarp off the beginning of a seascape. She closed her eyes and tried to see the rest of it, tried to feel that once-familiar pang to make it whole. There was nothing.

"No," she said aloud.

"What if you just tried? Here." Liza handed her a blank pad and pencils.

Jesse took them and stared at them. She set them on an already crowded table.

"I can't, Liza. I'm sorry."

"Okay. Let's get out of here."

They got back to the house, and Jesse sat on the couch, face in her hands.

"Let's go do something," Liza said. "Let's get out of the house. I'm starving. How about lunch?"

"I'm not really hungry."

"Well, shower and change anyway. You're going with me. I need to get food. You need to get out. Go get ready."

Jesse knew Liza was right. She stepped into the shower, her tears hidden in the flowing water. She took her time drying off, composing herself as she did. She took a deep, shaky breath and got dressed, then walked out to Liza.

"You okay, hon?" Liza said.

"I will be."

"It'll be good to get out, right?"

"Yeah. It should be."

"Good."

They went to an Italian restaurant in a southwest neighborhood. The food was good, but Jesse mostly moved hers around on her plate.

"What can I do to help you today?" Liza asked.

"I don't know. I'm sorry I'm such lousy company."

"Did you like the gal you took home last night? I mean, really like her? Are you feeling guilty?"

"No. Nothing like that. I mean, she was a lot of fun, don't get me wrong. But it wasn't anything special. I'm just missing Sara today. And nothing seems to be helping that."

"Talk to me. Maybe that'll help. Is today a special day? An anniversary or something?"

"Nope."

"Do you want to go see a movie or something after this? Maybe take your mind off her?"

"I don't think that'll work. I mean, thank you, but I think I just need to be alone."

"I hate the thought of that," Liza said.

"I know you do, but it's what I need today."

Liza dropped Jesse off after lunch.

"Call me if you need anything. Anything at all."

"I will. Thanks."

❖

Friday evening, Jesse drove home after a long, mundane day at work. She stopped by a fast food joint to get something to eat, since she wasn't in the mood to cook, which was the case more often than not lately. She got home and was contemplating her miserable life over a greasy burger. Liza was right. She needed more. It had been four years and she still felt as lousy as she did when she'd first lost Sara. Something had to change.

Obviously, it couldn't be her job. She might not work in the most exciting office, but it more than paid the bills, so she was pretty much stuck there. Besides, she couldn't imagine starting over at her age.

A relationship was also not going to happen. She was nowhere ready for that. So Liza was right. She needed a hobby or an interest. Her art was the logical choice. She made up her mind to try it out and see how she did. She walked out to her studio and braced herself anew.

The scents assaulted her and she almost walked out. She told herself to be strong, but felt her resolve waver. She quickly grabbed the sketch pad and pencils Liza had brought and left the building.

Jesse sat at her kitchen table, staring at her supplies. She opened the pencils and took a whiff of them. The familiarity was comforting, not terrifying. She flipped open the sketch pad. So, she had started. Now what to draw. The image of Sara standing at the window floated through her mind. That last moment when everything was normal right before she collapsed. She felt the need to capture it.

She picked up a pencil and started with the curtain bar and curtains. She had one curtain pulled back. She drew Sara's hand holding back the curtain. Jesse loved Sara's hands. They were soft and smooth, her fingers long and limber. She remembered the hours of pleasure they'd provided her, as well as how right they felt interlocked with her own.

Jesse remembered how Sara had looked that morning as she gazed at the birds flitting about their garden. She was so happy, her face so peaceful in the morning light. Neither of them knew that her life would end moments later.

Jesse sketched the outline of Sara's face, then added in the shadows of the sunlight as it played across her lovely features. She looked at the work she had done. It was good. She had to admit it. But the memories were too powerful for her to continue. She closed her sketchpad and went to bed.

The next morning, her phone rang at ten. She saw it was Liza.

"Good morning."

"Are you still in bed?" Liza said.

"Yeah. I was up late."

"What were you doing?"

"Honestly? I was drawing."

"Yeah. Good for you. I'm on my way over to see what you did."

The line went dead before Jesse could protest.

"Shit," she mumbled. She got out of bed and went to look at her work. Sure, it had looked good the night before, but what would it look like in the light of day?

It still looked good and Jesse was suitably impressed.

Liza showed up shortly thereafter and let herself in.

"I'm so excited. Let's go out back so I can see what you did."

"I couldn't work out there. I drew at the kitchen table." She handed Liza the pad.

"Oh my God, Jess. This is really good. When are you going to finish it?"

"I don't know that I will."

"Why not? It's amazing."

"It's Sara." Jesse said.

"So I see. You need to finish it. You caught her so perfectly."

"It's from her last minutes. She was looking out at the garden right before the brain aneurysm hit."

"Aw, hon. I'm sorry. But it's beautiful. And what a wonderful tribute to her."

"I suppose that's one way to look at it."

"It is. Now go get dressed." Liza said.

"Why?"

"Since the studio is so painful for you, we need to go buy you fresh supplies to use in here. Although I suppose painting in your kitchen isn't a good idea. What about the sun-room? That's better ventilated, isn't it?"

"Whoa. Slow down, sister. One step at a time."

"Okay, well, first, let's go get you supplies. I'm so happy you're getting back into your creative side. What prompted this anyway?"

"I just realized you were right," Jesse said. "I need something to do. I'm not getting any better just sitting around. I need an outlet."

"Good for you. Now get in the shower."

Jesse realized she was feeling better than she had in a long time as she showered. The prospect of shopping for art supplies lifted her spirits more than she'd imagined it could. She was happy to have her art back and was looking forward to seeing what else she could come up with.

They went to Jesse's favorite art store, only to find it had closed down.

"Well, that's depressing," she said.

"Nonsense. It's only a minor setback. Houston has to have lots of art supply stores. We'll find another one." Liza pulled out her phone and started searching. They found one located several blocks west and headed over.

They walked inside and Jesse at once felt at home.

"You gonna be okay?" Liza asked.

"Surprisingly, yes. I like being here."

They wandered through the aisles and Jesse was like a kid in a candy store. She stopped to look at every type of supply they had, even the pottery supplies, which she never used. Liza followed along behind her, checking things out and seeming to enjoy herself as well.

Jesse finally made her way to the paint section.

"Oh my God! Look at all this stuff," she said. "I want one of everything."

"Then get it. This is all for you. What do you want? Let's start collecting things."

"I don't even know where to start!"

"Let's start with the basics then. But you'll have to tell me what those are. I'm clueless."

"Acrylics. Definitely acrylics. And water paints and oils and canvasses and…" She looked around her, mesmerized by everything around her.

"Okay, okay. Slow down, sister. Where are the acrylics?"

Jesse grabbed an assortment of acrylics and put it in the cart. She added a couple of palettes to mix the paints on.

"I don't really need water colors or oils, I suppose."

"But what if you decide to use them? Better to have them," Liza said.

"You're right." She tossed some in the cart. "Now, we need brushes."

Liza watched patiently as Jesse scoured the selection of brushes, selecting only the finest to buy.

"I'm sorry. You must be bored out of your mind," Jesse said.

"Nonsense. I love seeing you like this. I'm having a blast. What about easels?"

"I've got plenty of easels."

"Um, Jess? You have easels, but they're in the studio."

Jesse paused, the reality of the statement sinking in.

"I can do this," she said. "You'll help me, right? We'll get them in the house and set up shop."

"Of course I'll help you," Liza said. "I'll bring them into the house for you."

"Thanks. You're a pal."

They checked out and Jesse didn't bat an eyelash at the cost of her new goodies.

"Let's get some food. I'm famished," Jesse said. "My treat."

"Sounds good to me."

It was early afternoon, but Jesse was craving meat and potatoes so they drove to a steak house where she bought them a huge lunch that cost her another small fortune. She didn't care. She was feeling better than she had in years. Literally. She was excited about the prospect of painting again. Sketching was fun, but painting was her passion.

After lunch, Liza took the easels out of the studio and Jesse set them up in her sun room. She moved some tables around and got everything set up with the best lighting possible. Liza left Jesse to her work. Jesse barely heard her leave.

CHAPTER THREE

Jesse woke up Sunday full of energy. She went to her cupboard to make coffee, then realized she was out. She needed to go shopping. A necessary evil, one she and Sara had always undertaken together. Since Sara died, Jesse only stopped by the store when absolutely necessary and never for more than just a few items. She wondered if it was time to try a full trip. No, she wasn't ready. She told herself she'd paint for a while then go pick up a few things.

She put a blank canvas on the easel and marveled at its beauty. It might look like nothing to most people, but to her it was a beginning, the start of something that would soon be the object of admiration.

She got out her acrylics and squeezed several colors on the palette. She used her palette knife to mix the colors until she had the perfect shade of blue. The blues and greens mixed with the slightest hint of yellow gave her the perfect color for the sea. She dipped her brush into the creation and moved it gracefully over the canvas. A swish here, a swoosh there, and she had the feeling of waves. The hint of yellow made her feel like she could see the sun shining on that spot.

Liza coughed quietly and Jesse turned.

"Good morning." Liza handed Jesse a cup of coffee from their favorite drive-thru.

"Thanks." Jesse took it gratefully and took a sip of the Caramel Delight. "I so needed this."

"Happy to help," Liza said. "You're at it early."

"I am. I'm so happy. Thank you for making me do this, Liza."

"I didn't make you do anything. I merely suggested you try something to keep yourself busy. This is your doing." She pointed to the area of paint on the canvas. "What's this going to be?"

"A seascape." Jesse laughed. She thought it was obvious, but realized she was seeing more in her mind's eye than what had actually already been painted.

"What's so funny? I'm supposed to guess that from a few strokes?"

"No, it's all good."

"Well, I won't keep you. I just wanted to check in and bring you some coffee. Let me know if you want to get together later."

"You know, Liza, you could always just call."

"You've been telling me that for four years. And you know I'm always going to stop by and check on you. It's what I do."

"Well, thank you for that. Come on in and sit a while."

"Nope. I'll let you get back to that. Next time I'm here I want to see the finished product."

"That you shall, my friend."

"Excellent." She stood silently for a minute. "You look good, Jess."

"Thanks. I feel good. Well, better, anyway."

"That makes me happy. Okay. I'm out of here. Do you need anything?"

"No. I'll work for a while then take care of what I need to."

"Sounds good to me. I'll talk to you later."

Liza left and Jesse went back to work.

She finished the ocean and left it to dry while she went to the store. She'd work on the sky and the boat over the next few days. She was feeling better every minute.

❖

The week dragged on for Jesse. Work was horrible. It was a boring job, and she was surrounded by petty, small-minded coworkers. Even the managers were idiots. She was smarter than any of them, and it killed her to watch all the drone employees fall at management's feet in worship.

She spent several nights sketching, since she didn't have the lighting all set up how she wanted it in the sunroom. It was good for daytime work, but not for night painting. So, she sketched. She finished several pieces and was happy with them, but by the end of the week, the usual depression had set in again and she found it hard to do anything. The only thing that kept her going was the promise of the dance on Saturday night.

Saturday evening finally arrived, and she took a long, hot shower, letting the water relieve the tensions of the week. She got out of the shower to find Liza standing in her living room, a bottle of tequila in one hand and a bottle of wine in the other.

"What are you in the mood for?" Liza asked.

"A little privacy?" Jesse joked.

"Since when do I give you that? Get dressed, stud muffin. I'll pour the shots."

"If you're doing shots, who's driving?" Jesse asked.

"We're taking a cab tonight. I want to let loose."

"Will Clancy be taking you home tonight?"

"That's the plan."

"Sounds good to me."

"Good. Then go get dressed. The sight of you in boxers and an undershirt does nothing for me, sorry to tell you."

"Oh, my. Aren't you in a mood tonight?" Jesse said.

"That I am."

Jesse went back to her room and finished dressing. She put on tan cargo pants and a black button-down shirt. She knew she looked good as she went out to join Liza. They each did a couple of shots, then called a cab. They did a couple more while they waited for the cab to get there. Jesse settled in to drinking a beer just as the cab arrived.

"We are going to have so much fun tonight," Liza said.

"That we are. I'm really looking forward to it."

They arrived at the bar to find the parking lot full.

"Looks like a good crowd tonight," Liza said.

"Right on. I love me a smorgasbord."

"You are so bad."

"But you love me that way."

The venue was darker than they were used to and it took Jesse's eyes a minute to adjust to it and take in the scene. The bar was along the west wall with the dance floor off to the right. Booths lined the walls, but there were tables set up practically on top of the dance floor. She scoped out the perfect table.

"Go get that table. I'll buy the first round," she said into Liza's ear. Liza walked off and Jesse went to the bar to get their drinks. She was already feeling very little pain from the tequila, but knew she'd soon be dancing it all out of her system.

Jesse got to the table and immediately heard a voice in her ear and felt the press of an ample bosom in her back.

"Hey, good lookin', how about a dance?"

She turned to see the woman from the previous dance standing there, though she couldn't remember her name.

"Hey, you. How are you tonight?"

"I'm good. Now, about that dance?"

"Sure. One dance won't hurt."

"Hey, I told you, I'm not the marrying kind. Relax. Let's dance."

Jesse followed her to the dance floor, loving the shape of her ass. When she turned to her, she got to see the outfit she was wearing. It was a black skirt with a blouse unbuttoned enough to show off her full cleavage.

"You look great tonight," Jesse said.

"Thanks. I thought you'd like this. You look quite stunning yourself."

"Thanks."

The dance went quickly and Jesse turned to leave the dance floor.

"So, I'm guessing we're a no go for tonight?" Chanelle said.

"It's a little early for that, isn't it?" Jesse said.

"Sure. Just keep me in mind as an option. If I haven't found someone else by the time you've decided."

Jesse shook her head as she got back to her table.

"What was that all about?" Liza asked.

Jesse recounted the exchange.

"I'm not into repeats," she said.

"Repeats don't make relationships," Liza said.

"But I don't want to lead her on. I'm not about to settle down with anyone."

"That's decent of you."

"Where's Clancy?"

"Running late. She'll be here, though."

"Good."

Jesse scanned the room, looking for someone to ask to dance. Her gaze lighted on a nice looking brunette in a form-fitting red dress.

"Oh, my God. I found who I'm taking home tonight."

"Who?" Liza turned.

"Don't look. Jeez, be cool, woman. You'll see her on the dance floor with me in just a second."

Jesse crossed the room confidently and reached the woman's table. She was taken aback briefly to see Chanelle sitting at the same table.

"Change your mind?" Chanelle asked.

"Actually," Jesse felt distinctly uncomfortable. "I was hoping your friend here would want to dance."

The woman stood and towered over Jesse. She had to be over six feet tall.

"Sure. I'd love to."

Jesse was undaunted by the woman's height. She was sure she could handle her.

"My name's Jesse."

"I'm Sylvia."

"Sylvia. Pretty name for a pretty lady."

"Thank you."

They danced several songs before Jesse walked Sylvia back to her table. She noticed with relief that Chanelle wasn't sitting there and hoped she'd found someone new to stalk.

Jesse returned to her table to find it empty. She looked out over the dance floor and saw Liza dancing with a tall, thin butch, definitely not Clancy. Jesse smiled to herself. Life was good. She signaled the waitress for two more drinks and took a pull of her beer.

"You look too good to be standing here alone," a voice said in her ear.

She turned to find an attractive redhead smiling at her.

"Would you care to join me?" Jesse asked.

"Sure. I'll have a martini."

Jesse laughed at the woman's boldness.

"One martini coming up." She pushed through to the bar and back to the table. She handed the drink to the woman.

"This is perfect," she said.

"Good. I'm Jesse, by the way."

"I'm Katie."

"Nice to meet you, Katie."

"Oh, believe me, the pleasure is all mine."

Jesse stared into Katie's blue eyes and saw a desire burning there that made her wet.

"Would you like to dance?" Jesse asked.

"I'd love to."

They made their way to the center of the floor and moved in time with the music. Soon Jesse realized that Katie was unaware of everything around her as she gyrated in time with the music. Jesse barely moved as she watched Katie's body ebb and flow with the beat. It was the most sensual dance Jesse had ever witnessed. She knew Katie would be hot in the bedroom and was happy she'd sought her out.

The music slowed and Katie took Jesse's hand and placed it around her body.

"Hold me tight, tiger."

Jesse was happy to oblige. She pulled Katie close and relished the feel of her soft body against her own. Katie wasn't as curvy as Chanelle had been, but she was definitely all woman and Jesse couldn't wait to get her naked.

They walked back to their table to find Liza all alone.

"I'm sorry," Katie stuttered. "I didn't realize you were with someone."

"Oh, it's not like that," Liza said. "We're just friends. I'm Liza."

"I'm Katie. And are you sure I'm not intruding?"

"Positive." Jesse kept her arm possessively around Katie's waist.

"Good. Because I really like you."

"I really like you, too."

They finished their drinks and danced some more. By the time they got back to their table, Clancy had shown up and she and Liza were in a passionate lip lock.

"They have the right idea." Katie sidled up to Jesse and wrapped her arms around her neck.

Jesse smelled a hint of vanilla and a spice like cinnamon. It was a heady scent that left her dizzy with desire. She pressed Katie against her as she looked into her eyes, the same longing still there, only magnified. She lowered her mouth slowly, making herself wait for the inevitable rush that would come when their lips met. She wasn't disappointed. Katie's lips were soft and full, made for kissing. Jesse's heart skipped a beat and the desire she'd been feeling roared out of control.

She kissed her again, this time prying Katie's lips open with her tongue. When their tongues touched, Jesse's knees went weak. She didn't know how long she'd be able to stay at the dance. She wanted to get Katie home and to bed.

Katie broke the kiss and stepped back.

"Wow. You know what you're doing."

"So do you."

"We should enjoy our drinks and cool off, don't you think?"

"Or we could get out of here."

"Your place or mine?"

"Well, I don't have a car, do you?"

"I do."

"So, you drive and we'll head back to my place."

"Sounds good."

Katie kept up a constant flow of conversation as they drove.

"I can't believe I'm doing this."

"Doing what?"

"I don't know anything about you. How do I know you're not an axe murderer?"

"Would I have a friend like Liza if I was?" Jesse joked.

"How should I know?"

"Besides," Jesse said. "What do you need to know about me? You want me. I want you. What's to know?"

"I do like that logic."

"So, do you not usually take women home from dances?" Jesse was getting nervous. She didn't want a clingon.

"Not usually. Do you?"

"Sure. If the opportunity presents itself."

"And how often does that happen?"

Jesse shrugged. She wasn't about to share that it happened almost every dance.

"Look," she said. "If you're having second thoughts, you can just drop me off at my house. I won't hold it against you."

"Are you crazy? And miss a shot with you? I'd be foolish."

"You know, just because we sleep together doesn't make a relationship."

"Oh, I know. Don't worry."

"Okay, good." Jesse breathed a sigh of relief.

They got to her house and she was determined to get the mood back. She walked Katie back to her room and lit some candles.

"How romantic," Katie said.

"I want you to relax," Jesse said.

"Oh, honey, I'm anything but relaxed. But it's not a bad thing."

"You seemed a little nervous in the car."

"Just a little. I don't do this often, like I said."

"But think back to when you hit on me. You knew then you wanted me."

"I did. And I do." She moved closer to Jesse. "I do big time."

Jesse closed the distance between them and kissed her softly.

"See? It's all going to be okay."

"Yes, it is. Kiss me again."

Jesse was happy to oblige and kissed Katie so passionately, she felt her knees give out. She eased her down on the bed. She kissed her again as she lay down on top of her, feeling her soft curves under her.

"You have the most amazing body," Jesse said.

Katie didn't answer, just kissed her harder and wrapped her legs around Jesse, pressing her into her. Jesse felt the heat from Katie's center and it drove her wild. She wanted her desperately and ground into her.

Jesse slipped her hand between them and cupped a firm breast. She lightly squeezed it and elicited a slight moan from Katie.

"I mean it," she said. "Your body is smokin'."

"I'm so glad you like it," Katie said. "Yours is pretty hot, too."

"Let's get out of these clothes. I want all of you."

They stood and stripped, then lay back down. Jesse was surprised when Katie rolled her over on her back.

"Now, let me at you."

"Huh? Ladies first," Jesse said.

"Not tonight, tiger. I'm gonna fuck you senseless."

Jesse tried to argue, but Katie was kissing her again while she dragged her hand between Jesse's legs.

"Oh, shit, that feels good." Jesse didn't want her to stop. She arched her back, encouraging her to explore more.

"You like that, huh? What about this?"

Katie moved her fingers inside Jesse and pressed them as deep as they would go. She moved her fingers around while Jesse moved against her.

"Holy fuck, yes," Jesse said. "Oh dear God!"

She was lost in the moment, focusing only on the feel of Katie's fingers deep inside her. She hadn't been that filled in a long time. She reveled in the feeling as she rode her hand, each buck bringing her closer and closer to her release.

Katie moved her thumb so it brushed Jesse's protruding clit and Jesse felt her world somersault as she came hard and fast.

"Oh, sister. You sure know how to please a woman."

"I'm not through yet."

"Oh yes, you are. It's my turn now." She fought to find her energy to roll over and pin Katie on her back.

"No," Katie said. "Not like this."

She rolled over to her stomach and got on all fours.

"I want you to fuck me like this. From behind. That way I'll feel your fingers in my throat."

Jesse laughed at her description. But she knew she could get deeper if she entered her from behind and the sight of Katie on her hands and knees waiting for her got her wet anew. She stared at that shapely ass in the air for her playtime and knew she couldn't say no.

"Now would be good," Katie said, looking back over her shoulder.

Jesse kissed Katie's shoulders, nibbling and sucking them. She kissed down her back and finally kissed one butt cheek and then the other. She was soft and smooth and totally fuckable. Jesse slid her hand between Katie's legs. She found her wet and swollen. She rubbed her clit and Katie mewled.

"You're so ready for me," Jesse said.

"God, yes, I am. Please don't make me wait any longer."

Jesse moved her fingers inside Katie and plunged them as deep as they could go.

"Yes, yes. That's it."

Jesse continued what she was doing, biting Katie's ass as she fucked her.

"Harder. Harder, please," Katie whined.

Jesse didn't know how hard to go. She didn't want to hurt Katie, but she certainly wanted to please her. She bent over her, pressing her own breasts into Katie's back and used her hips to drive her hand deeper.

"Oh fuck that feels good. Oh God, yes. Yes, Jesse, oh God yes."

She collapsed onto her elbows as the orgasm hit. Jesse kept her hand in deep while Katie clamped around it, pulsating over and over. When Katie finally released her fingers, Jesse rolled off her and fell onto her back, exhausted from her workout.

"You were something else, woman."

"Thanks. I love it like that, but I'm always embarrassed to ask for it. I figured you wouldn't care."

"Not at all. Anything goes on a one-night stand."

"A one-night stand?"

"Yeah. You meet someone at a dance and take them home. You have a good time. Nothing wrong with that."

"True. I just thought…"

Jesse sat up.

"Oh, Katie. I thought you understood." She could see the disappointment on Katie's face. "Look, hon, you're a real sweet woman. Someone's going to want you for their partner. But I'm not the settling down kind. I'm really sorry."

"It's because of what I asked you to do to me, isn't it? You think I'm gross."

"Not at all. That was fuckin' hot. I just don't want a relationship right now."

"Whatever. I'm leaving."

Jesse knew she should say something, ask her to stay, but she wanted her to leave. She didn't want her to stay the night. Still, she felt bad.

"Look, you're really swell. I mean that. I had a lot of fun. Didn't you?"

"Like you care."

"I do."

"Yes. I had fun. You're a great lover. Add me to your dossier."

Katie had finished dressing.

"I'll see myself out."

Jesse heard her front door close. She got up and locked it and climbed back in bed, the thrill of the evening already wearing off.

Chapter Four

J esse was still in bed the next day when Liza showed up.
"Hey, sleepy head. What are you doing?"
"I don't want to get up."
"No? I thought I'd find you hard at work."
"I don't feel like it."
Liza sat on the bed.
"I'm sorry, kiddo. Rough day? Or rough night?"
"Both. I just don't want to get out of bed today. I'll be okay. I'll just sleep the day away."
"I don't think so. Look what I found." She handed Jesse a newspaper clipping.
Jesse took the clipping. It was for an art show in the park the following month. She felt a twinge of excitement, then set the clipping down.
"I'll never be ready. Besides, I probably missed the sign up period."
"The sign up period ends today and I already signed you up."
Jesse sat up.
"You what? Liza, I'm not ready for a show."
"Come on. It's not like a 'show' show. It's a bunch of artists out in the park on a spring day showing off their wares. Very low key. And just the perfect place for you to get a little exposure."
"I've never done anything like this."
"You'll be fine. And I'll be with you. It'll be fun. Now get up and get to work."

Jesse lay back down and pulled the covers over her head.
"No."

"Fine. Suit yourself. But there'll be a place with your name on it at the park next month and you'll look pretty stupid if you don't show up."

Jesse lowered the covers and looked at her.

"You're really going to make me do this, aren't you?"

"I am. I think it'll be a great opportunity for you. And what if your art took off? And you could quit your job and be a full-time artist?"

"Whoa!" Jesse had to laugh. "Easy there, turbo. One step at a time. How about I get out of bed today? That is an accomplishment in and of itself. Let's not go making me the next Georgia O'Keefe."

"Oh you won't be."

"There's the confidence I've come to rely on."

"No. You won't be Georgia O'Keefe because you don't paint hoo-has."

"Hoo-has? Did you just really say that?"

"I did."

Jesse was laughing despite herself.

"Okay. Move. I'll get up. Did you bring me coffee?"

"Don't I always?"

Jesse put her feet on the floor. It was a good first step. She reached for the cup of coffee on the nightstand and took a sip. It felt wonderful going down.

"So how was last night?" Liza asked.

"Oh, Christ. Don't ask."

"That good, huh? Did you strike out?"

"No, just broke her heart."

"Yeah, right."

"No, she didn't like the idea it was a one-night stand. She got all pissy with me."

"Well, that's not the first time that's happened."

"Doesn't mean I have to like it."

"True."

Jesse padded to her dresser and pulled out some sweats.

"I guess I should get started if I'm going to have anything to show at this gig you've signed me up for."

"I guess you should. Show me what you already have again."

Jesse had several paintings done, mostly seascapes and a variety of sketches.

"What happened to that first sketch you were working on?" Liza asked. "The one of Sara."

"No. I can't finish it."

"It was beautiful, Jess. I think you should take it to the show."

"I don't want anyone else to have it. It's for me. If I ever decide to finish it."

"Well, do one similar to it to take to the show. I think you have enough already. I mean they don't give y'all a lot of space to show your stuff at these things. So it's not like you have to go crazy and paint a bunch of more stuff."

"No. You're right. Maybe one more painting. I have an idea for one."

"Okay, well, you get to it. I'll catch you later."

"See ya."

Jesse got out her palette and squeezed some paints on it. She started with all green. She applied the green to the canvas and immediately felt better. She could already see it taking shape. She mixed some blue in and painted a section with the darker color. She was pleased with what she was doing. She continued to work, and when the landscape portion was complete, left it to dry before she finished the rest of it.

She grabbed a beer and sat on the couch. An hour and a half later, she realized she was still on the couch, staring absently at the television. She had no idea what was on or what had been on before. She had been lost in thought, remembering happier days.

Her painting forgotten, she grabbed another beer and tried to drink away the pain.

Sunday morning, Jesse was already up and cleaning her house when Liza arrived.

"Oh, good. I'm glad to see you're up and at 'em. Though, you look a little the worse for wear," Liza said.

"I had a date with the Patron you left here," Jesse admitted.

"Oh, no. I thought you'd be working on your art."

"I was. Then I stopped for a break and then it was all over."

"That bites. But you're cleaning today. That's a good sign."

"It's got to be done."

"Yes, it does."

"So, guess what I have?" Liza said.

"Chlamydia?"

"Aren't you funny? No, you asshole. I got us Square Register."

"A who what?"

"It's an app that lets us collect money from people at the show. They can swipe their cards and we get money. We just need to get it all set up."

"You think I'm going to sell something, don't you?"

"I think you'll be surprised."

"So, cool. You're going to be there collecting money, huh?"

"I wouldn't make you go through this alone."

"Thanks."

"Now go get dressed and let's get some food."

❖

St. Patrick's Day arrived and Jesse was feeling good. She had actually started looking forward to the art show coming up in a couple of weeks. And the night brought a huge celebration at The Black Hole. She was getting dressed when Liza showed up, looking like the true St. Patrick's Day fan that she was. Even her tennis shoes were green. Although, Jesse thought she looked ridiculous with the green antennae on her head.

But Liza had brought a six-pack of Guinness, so Jesse wasn't going to complain. She grabbed one and sat on the couch.

"Tonight's going to be a blast," she said. "Is Clancy going to be there?"

"Nope. I'm flying solo tonight. But I don't plan to end the night that way."

"Hear, hear."

They each finished their beer and headed to the bar. It was early, only seven thirty, but the place was packed.

"I hope there's still some corned beef," Jesse said as they walked in.

"I'm sure there will be. This place is famous for their St. Patrick's Day Corned Beef Feed. They're usually still serving until later when people get the drunkchies."

They smelled the food and Jesse's stomach growled.

"Man, I'm starving. Let's get some food."

They got plates and found an empty table.

Jesse scouted the place as she ate.

"There are a lot of choices here tonight," she said.

"You're telling me. I'm in heaven."

While they were eating, Liza brought up the art show.

"So, how are you feeling about it? Are you going to be able to do it?"

"Yeah. I'm actually looking forward to it."

"Really? That makes me so happy."

"Really. Thanks again for talking me into getting back into my art."

"My pleasure. It's good for you and you're so good at it," Liza said.

"Well, we'll see what the rest of Houston thinks in a couple of weeks."

"Yes, we will."

They finished dinner and Jesse sat back with her Guinness to let her food digest.

"What are you doing? We're here to prowl. You look like you're content to just sit here," Liza said.

"Jesus, woman. Give me a minute to let things settle. I'd hate to puke on a dance partner."

"Well, I don't plan to waste any time. I'm going to get my groove on. I'll catch up with you later."

Liza was back within fifteen minutes.

"What's the haps? I thought you were going to be makin' it by now," Jesse said.

"There are a lot of couples here tonight."

"No way. All these women and they're all in relationships? That can't be right."

"It sure seemed that way to me."

"Well, we'll wait a while. More people will show up."

They sat at their table, enjoying their drinks and keeping a constant focus on the patrons. They did seem to be paired up, but neither was worried. They relaxed and watched the dancers.

After an hour had passed, more people started to arrive. They watched the newcomers with interest and were happy to note that most arrived in groups or alone, but very few came in as couples.

"Now it's getting interesting," Jesse said.

"Yes, it is. Has your dinner settled yet, because I think it's time we start tearing it up."

"It has indeed. Let's do this."

They left their drinks on the table and each took a different side of the dance floor. Jesse was halfway around the floor when she noticed Sylvia from the last dance she'd been to.

"Hey, lady. How are you? Would you like to dance?"

"Sure." Sylvia stood. "Somehow I never thought I'd see you again."

"Why's that?"

"We danced, we laughed, and you disappeared."

"Sorry about that. It was nothing personal, I assure you."

"Good."

They danced a few dances and Jesse walked her back to her table.

"Can I buy you a drink?"

"Sure. I'd like a lemon drop."

"That's not very Irish."

"I'm not very Irish." Sylvia smiled.

"Fair enough."

Jesse came back from the bar to find Sylvia on the dance floor. Oh well, she didn't own her. She sat and enjoyed watching her tall figure move to the music. She knew how to use what the good Lord gave her. That was for sure.

Sylvia came back and sat next to her.

"Sorry. I love to dance."

"No worries. I love to watch you dance, so we're even."

"You're a smooth talker, Jesse."

"Maybe I'm a smooth operator."

"I get the feeling you are."

"Is that a problem?"

"I'll have to get back to you on that."

"Would you like to dance again?"

"Sure."

Jesse led her back to the floor and they moved as one to the pulsating rhythm. Jesse loved how comfortable Sylvia was to be around and how genuinely lost she got in the music. When several songs had played and the last one was ending, Jesse stopped dancing. She watched Sylvia with her head thrown back, eyes closed, squeezing the last few steps out of the music. Jesse couldn't resist; she kissed Sylvia's exposed neck. It tasted salty yet sweet, and she smelled of expensive perfume. Jesse wondered if she might not be the one-night stand type. It wasn't too late for Jesse to look elsewhere for a bedmate for the night. But she was intrigued by Sylvia.

Sylvia opened her eyes when Jesse's lips met her neck. Her head snapped down and she stared at Jesse. Jesse wondered if she'd gone too far. She looked at Sylvia expectantly and breathed a sigh of relief at the slow smile that spread across her face.

"I need to keep my eye on you, don't I?" Sylvia said.

"I suppose you might."

They walked back to the table and sat down. Sylvia put her hand on Jesse's thigh. Jesse covered it with her own. Her skin was soft and smooth, just as she imagined the rest of her would be.

Sylvia slid her hand away and moved it slowly up Jesse's leg.

Jesse steeled herself, wondering how far Sylvia would go.

"Your legs are solid. Do you work out?" Sylvia said.

"I used to. Not so much anymore."

"Well, then you're blessed with wonderful genes."

"Thank you."

Sylvia seemed content to rest her hand just shy of where Jesse's legs met. Jesse was tempted to shift her position to create contact but held back. Not only was she still not sure about Sylvia, she was in a public place.

"So, what's your story?" Sylvia asked.

"What do you mean?"

"You just make the rounds hitting on women? How come no nice lady has scooped you up?"

"I'm not really looking to settle down." There. She'd said it. Let Sylvia decide for herself about the rest of the night.

"No? Why not?"

"Been there. Done that. Don't need it right now."

"I hear ya. Bad breakup, huh?"

"Something like that."

Jesse was decidedly uncomfortable with the conversation, so tried as smoothly as she could to turn the tables.

"And you? You just cruise the circuit, too?"

"I'm looking for Ms. Right."

"I'm sorry, Sylvia. I'm not that person."

"Oh, I know. I can tell. But you might just be Ms. Right for the night, which works for some of us lonely women."

Jesse felt the relief wash over her. This just might work out, after all.

"Lonely? You? I'm sure you have women beating a path to your door."

"That's awfully kind of you to say. But it's not easy being single when you don't want to be."

"Well, hooking up with me isn't going to help your chances of finding Ms. Right tonight."

"That's okay. Like I said, a night with you will be all I need for now."

"So how else do you try to meet women?"

"Why? You need tips?" Sylvia laughed.

"Heck no! Not interested. Just looking out for you."

"How about if we stop talking and dance some more?"

"That sounds good."

The song was slow and Sylvia felt wonderful in Jesse's arms. She was tall, but not as tall as she'd first appeared. They fit together nicely and moved well together to the beat.

"Would you like another drink?" Jesse asked.

"Why don't we get out of here?" Sylvia said.

"Sounds good to me."

They walked hand-in-hand to the parking lot and arrived at Sylvia's car. Jesse pressed her against it and kissed her, hard. Sylvia kissed back with a ferocity Jesse had only dreamed of. Her hands were in Jesse's hair, her tongue in her mouth, her leg between Jesse's. It was a kiss that made Jesse's head swim.

"Wow."

"Not bad, huh?" Sylvia said.

"That's a bit of an understatement."

"Come on. Let's get you home."

They climbed into the car and Sylvia pulled Jesse to her again. The kiss was long and passionate, almost desperate with the amount of need put into it. Jesse wanted to climb over the console and devour Sylvia, but she pulled back and settled into her seat. The night held all sorts of promise.

They arrived at Jesse's place and Jesse was ready to take off where the last kiss had ended, but Sylvia seemed to have cooled. She looked around the entrance hall.

"This is nice. I like the artwork. Who is it?"

"It's me. I dabble once in a while."

"Impressive."

"Thank you." She wanted nothing less than to ravish Sylvia and was frustrated at the mixed signals she was picking up. "Did you want something to drink?"

"What do you have?"

"Not much. Tequila and beer, essentially."

"Anything to mix with that tequila?"

Jesse wanted to say no so they'd have to just go to bed, but she couldn't do that.

"I have grapefruit juice."

"I'll have a tequila and grapefruit juice."

"Coming right up," Jesse said. "Oh. This way to the living room. Have a seat."

She went to the kitchen and came back with the drink and another Guinness for herself. She sat next to Sylvia on the couch.

"How's your drink?"

"It's very good. Thank you."

Sylvia set her drink down and turned to face Jesse.

"How's your beer?"

"It's not my favorite, but it's Irish, so I've gotta drink it today."

"You take St. Patrick's Day seriously, don't you?"

"I do! It's all in fun."

Sylvia reached out and stroked Jesse's jaw. Jesse felt the touch all the way to her clit.

"You're a very sexy woman, Jesse. Do you know that?"

"I'm certainly glad you think so. Because you exude sensuality."

"Really? I think we're going to have a wonderful night, don't you?"

Jesse leaned in and kissed Sylvia. The kiss was fiery and Jesse was surprised as Sylvia eased her onto her back and climbed on top of her. She felt Sylvia's hand on her breast and gasped when she pinched her nipple. She wasn't used to letting someone else take charge, but it seemed that's what Sylvia had in mind and she wasn't going to complain.

Their kissing continued, mouths wide and tongues tangled. Jesse brought her knee between Sylvia's legs. Sylvia ground into her, and Jesse needed more.

"Let's get out of these clothes," Jesse said.

"Patience," Sylvia said.

Jesse was breathing heavily and didn't want to wait any longer. She didn't know how long she'd last. She was already about to explode.

"I don't have much patience," Jesse breathed.

"Ah. I think you do."

Sylvia untucked Jesse's shirt. She ran her hand over her stomach.

"Your body is so nice. I can't believe you don't work out."

Jesse didn't respond. She was holding her breath, every touch accentuating her frustration.

Sylvia moved between Jesse's legs and kissed her belly. Jesse needed her mouth elsewhere.

"You're killing me."

"But what a way to go, huh?"

She pushed up Jesse's shirt, kissing and licking as she went. She finally eased the shirt over Jesse's head as she closed her mouth around a nipple.

"Oh God," Jesse moaned. She watched Sylvia's obvious enjoyment as she suckled. The sight flamed the fire already threatening to consume her.

Sylvia released her grip on Jesse and kissed her mouth, another passionate kiss that left Jesse dizzy. Jesse could take no more. She managed to slide out from underneath Sylvia and stand on shaky legs. She reached a hand out and pulled Sylvia up to join her.

They kissed again before Jesse took Sylvia back to her bedroom.

"I'm going to have my way with you now," Jesse said. She lay down, facing Sylvia. As they kissed, she ran her hand over the length of her body, stopping to unbutton her slacks. She lowered the zipper before moving her hand back up to cup a breast.

Sylvia took her blouse off and Jesse unhooked her bra. Her breasts sprang free and Jesse greedily grabbed them. She fondled both of them, running her thumbs over the hardened nipples. She took one in her mouth while Sylvia pushed her slacks down over her hips.

Jesse moved her hand below Sylvia's belly and felt lace. She looked down and saw black lacy panties.

"Those are sexy as all hell," Jesse said.

"I hope you don't expect me to wear them long."

"No chance of that." She wriggled her fingers inside the waistband and felt the heat radiating from Sylvia's center. She peeled the panties off Sylvia and spread her legs. She moved her hand all over her, coating it in Sylvia's essence. She coated Sylvia's nipples with her juices and bent to suck on them.

"You taste amazing," she said. "But I knew you would."

She kissed her on the mouth.

"See?"

"I do," Sylvia said.

Jesse ran her hand between Sylvia's legs and pressed it into her clit.

"Oh yeah. That's right," Sylvia said.

Jesse slid her fingers inside.

"Deeper, please. Deeper," Sylvia said.

Jesse was happy to oblige. She plunged her fingers as deep as they would go and moved them in and out.

Sylvia reached down and rubbed her clit while Jesse fucked her.

"Oh dear God. Oh God, yes," Sylvia said.

She screamed as she came, and Jesse was worried the neighbors might have heard.

Jesse took her fingers out and pressed them into Sylvia's clit. It didn't take any time before she cried out again.

Sylvia placed her hands on Jesse's cheeks and kissed her.

"My turn," she said.

She and Jesse worked together to get Jesse naked. She raked her fingernails all over Jesse's body, including over her pert nipples.

Jesse shivered. The sensations Sylvia was causing were amazing. She needed more and spread her legs. Sylvia dragged her fingernails over her exposed clit.

"Holy shit." Jesse couldn't believe everything she was feeling. She felt Sylvia's fingernails circling her opening and got scared. She was afraid they'd cut her if they went inside, but the feeling at the moment was arousing.

"Dear God, you're killing me. Finish me off. Please."

Sylvia moved back to Jesse's clit and scraped it gently. Jesse raised off the bed, needing harder contact. Finally, Sylvia pressed into her with her fingers, and Jesse felt her whole body tense. She was aware of nothing but the pressure building between her legs. With each circle, the pressure built until her very center exploded in a powerful gush of energy.

"Holy shit," Jesse said again when she could speak.

"I knew you'd be fun," Sylvia said.

"As were you."

"I like you, Jesse. I'm not going to lie to you. But I know there's nothing here."

Jesse was conflicted by the statement. It scared her, then relieved her, but she wasn't sure how relieved she should be.

"The point is," Sylvia went on. "I don't think it would be healthy for me to stay the night. I know in my head that it's a one-night stand, but my heart might dream up more if I sleep in your arms."

"I get what you're saying. Come on. Let's get dressed."

Jesse pulled on her boxers and undershirt and waited while Sylvia got dressed.

"Thanks for tonight, stud," Sylvia said.

"Thank you."

"I guess I'll see you around, huh?"

"I guess."

She saw Sylvia out then climbed into bed and fell into a restful sleep.

CHAPTER FIVE

Jesse barely got through the next two weeks. Her night with Sylvia was forgotten the minute she woke the next morning. And things went downhill from there. She didn't have any reason to paint, since she had more than enough for her show. Liza kept pushing her to work on new projects, but she didn't want to. She didn't want to do anything.

A week later, Liza found Jesse still in bed again.

"What's up with you? You've been in a bigger funk than usual," Liza said.

"I don't want to talk about it."

"Even to me? Come on. You tell me everything."

"Let it go."

"Jess? It'll help to talk."

Jesse fought to look mad but couldn't stop the tear that ran down her cheek.

"Jesse. Oh my God, what's wrong?"

Jesse drew a ragged breath. She thought about saying something, but didn't trust her voice. Instead, she rolled over and pulled the covers over her head, trying to compose herself. She couldn't though, she lost it and started bawling.

She just wanted to be left alone. She felt the pressure of Liza's hand on her back and knew she wasn't going anywhere. Part of her thought Liza should already know what was wrong, but part of her knew she was expecting too much. Why would Liza remember?

Liza gently pulled the covers down until she could see Jesse's face.

"You're really hurting. What the hell is going on?"

"She died today," Jesse said.

"What? Who? Oh, Sara? Oh, honey!"

Jesse allowed herself to be pulled into a hug while she continued to sob.

"I'm sorry I forgot the date," Liza said.

"It's okay. I didn't."

"No. I wouldn't expect you to."

"I know you're going to want me to go somewhere or do something, but I really can't today."

"No. I totally get that. I won't push you today. Is there anything I can do for you?"

"No, thanks. I'll just sleep. Or maybe mope around. I don't need anything."

"Well, I brought you a coffee."

"Thanks."

"And I can bring some food to you. You need to eat something."

"I'm fine. I'm not hungry."

"No, but you'll need food. I'll bring it later. I'll leave you now. Call if you need anything at all."

"Thanks."

Liza left and Jesse lay there, the pain in her heart as fresh as the day it happened. She punched her pillow, angry at the fates who had taken Sara so early and unfairly from her. She let out a wail as the pain and anger overwhelmed her. She buried her face in the pillow and cried herself back to sleep.

Jesse woke up several hours later to the smell of barbecue. She rolled over in bed, confused, but heard footsteps and figured Liza must have come back. She checked the clock. It was two o'clock. She'd slept for a while.

She got out of bed and pulled some sweats on. She walked to the kitchen and found Liza serving up the food. She walked right past her to the cabinet and grabbed the bottle of tequila. Liza gave her a look, which she ignored as she poured herself a shot.

"Are you seriously just getting up?" Liza asked.

"Don't judge."

"Not judging. Just worrying."

"I'm not hungry."

"I knew you wouldn't be. But I want you to eat some pulled pork, at least. You don't have to eat a whole lot."

"I don't have to eat anything."

"No, but you should."

Jesse knew Liza was right. She poured another shot then sat at the table.

"The alcohol will hit faster on an empty stomach, though."

"You don't want to puke. So don't even talk that way."

"I don't want to puke. Just be numb."

Liza set a plate in front of her.

"You can be numb without alcohol."

"Yeah, but it helps."

She took a bite of the pork. She had expected it to taste like cardboard, since she figured even her taste buds would be broken, but it was surprisingly good. She helped herself to some coleslaw and biscuits. She was hungrier than she'd thought.

"Wow. That's an appetite I didn't think you'd have."

"Yeah. Who knew? This stuff is really good. Thanks."

"My pleasure. Do you mind if I hang out for a while?"

"Aren't you gonna eat?"

"If you don't mind," Liza said.

"Not at all. Have a seat. But I don't promise to be good company."

"Fair enough. I don't expect you to be."

Jesse took another bite of food, then put her fork down as tears poured from her eyes.

"Damn it, Liza! It's not fair! She should still be here."

Liza reached out and took Jesse's hand in hers. She sat silently as Jesse sobbed.

"She didn't do anything wrong. She was a good person. She didn't deserve to die that young. And she had no warning. There was no way to prepare for it or fight it. It's so unfair!"

"You're right, Jesse," Liza said. "It was a horrible thing to happen."

"And there's nothing I can do to bring her back. I know this, but God I miss her, Liza. I miss her so fucking much."

Liza got out of her chair and pulled Jesse to her, letting her cry. Jesse wrapped her arms around her and held on for dear life, the sobs making it too hard to speak.

When she had cried herself out, she released her death grip on Liza.

"I think I need to go back to bed now," she said.

"Sure, kiddo. I'll get this cleaned up and I'll be back to check on you tomorrow."

Jesse climbed back into bed but couldn't sleep. She kept playing over the fateful morning that Sara was taken from her. They'd shared a passionate night of lovemaking and had slept in, since they'd both taken the day off as part of a weeklong vacation to work on the house.

Sara had poured them each a cup of coffee and Jesse watched Sara walk over to the window. She loved the garden and enjoyed watching the birds flit about it. Jesse couldn't take her eyes off Sara, who pulled back the curtain to gaze at her creation.

It was then that Sara let out a blood-curdling scream and fell to the floor. She was dead before the paramedics got there. It was determined that it was a brain aneurysm that had taken her life and there was nothing anyone could have done for her.

Present day Jesse cried harder, missing Sara like she was missing a part of her soul. She finally fell back to sleep and didn't wake until the following morning.

Eyes puffy and head pounding, Jesse got out of bed before Liza arrived with her coffee. She sat at the kitchen table, head in her hands. She still felt like crap and wanted to go back to bed, but knew she couldn't spend the rest of her life in bed. It had been four years, and Sara would want her to live a life that didn't involve darkness and sleep. She'd realized that a month after Sara died, as well, but every year on the anniversary, the urge to do just that came back.

She was trying to decide what to do first with her day when Liza waltzed in with coffee, which Jesse took gratefully.

"You look like shit, girlfriend," Liza said.

"Thanks. I still don't feel that hot."

"But better than yesterday?"

"I suppose. I'm making myself believe that, anyway."

"Good. Did you want to do anything today?"

"Ugh. I don't know."

"Okay. Just checking."

"I could use some new supplies. You feel like going supply shopping with me?"

"Sure. That would be fun. You sure you're up for it?"

"I think I have to be."

They did their shopping and Jesse felt a little better, until she got home. Suddenly, she was exhausted and just wanted to go to bed.

"Don't you want to try out any of your new products?" Liza asked.

"Not today. Maybe tomorrow."

"Ah, hon, I'm sorry you're not feeling well."

"I'll get over it. Sort of. I just need some down time now."

"Okay. I'll see myself out. Call me if you need anything."

Jesse didn't even put her new supplies in the sunroom. She simply stripped down and climbed into bed.

The work week was mundane, but at least it kept her mind somewhat occupied. And the closer it got to the weekend, the more excited she got about the show. She knew she had to shake her funk to be on her best game to sell her artwork.

Liza took her out to dinner Friday night.

"So, how you doing? You going to be ready for tomorrow?" Liza asked.

"I think so," Jesse said. She took a sip of her beer. "I feel better than I have in a while."

"In a week, anyway." Liza smiled.

"Well, yeah. Definitely the best I've felt all week."

"I'm glad. I'm so ready for tomorrow. We're going to have fun."

"Yeah, we are. And maybe sell a few things even, but definitely get my name out there. Thanks for doing this with me. I really appreciate that."

"My pleasure. You schmooze and I'll take the money. That works for me."

"Works for me, too."

They ate their dinner and Liza had Jesse home by ten.

"Get some sleep. We have to be there by eight tomorrow."

"No worries. I'll be ready when you get here."

"We'll see." Liza laughed.

Jesse went to bed but was too excited to sleep. She tossed and turned thinking about the day ahead of her. She finally fell asleep, where she was haunted by dreams of Sara.

She woke feeling anything but rested, but grateful the night's nightmares were over. She hopped in the shower and dressed in shorts and a golf shirt.

She was loading paintings into her truck when Liza got there.

"Hey there! Look who's up and at 'em early this morning."

"I'm so ready for this. I'm glad we picked up those extra easels last weekend. I'm going to need them all for my display."

"Can I help?"

"Nothing personal, but these are my babies. I really only trust myself to get them there in the best shape."

"No problem. Can you at least take a break for some coffee?"

Jesse checked her watch. It was seven o'clock.

"I suppose I have time for a sip or two."

Liza laughed and sat on a patio chair. Jesse joined her. She sipped her coffee. Nectar of the gods.

"This is good stuff. And just what I needed. Thank you."

"You're welcome. I can't believe you're already showered and ready and loading up. I thought for sure I'd have to pry you out of bed."

"Nope. I'm so excited, Liza. I can't tell you. I thought I would dread it, but I'm totally up for it."

"That's great!"

Jesse went back to loading her paintings then carefully placed her sketches on the passenger seat of her truck.

"I guess we're taking two cars then?" Liza said.

"Oh, yeah. Sorry, but we kind of have to."

"No worries. I'm just happy I get to be a part of this at all."

They arrived at the park and found their reserved spot. Jesse went to work setting up her art, making sure each was situated in its best light. She knew she'd have to change the positioning as the light changed through the day, but she was still determined to have everything at its very best.

Liza went off in search of chairs for them. By the time she got back, Jesse had everything just the way she wanted it.

"Looks amazing, my friend," Liza said.

"Thanks. Let's just hope others feel that way."

"So what do we do now?" Liza said.

"We wait. I'm gonna cruise around for a bit. You mind holding down the fort?"

"Not at all."

Jesse wandered to the section next to hers. The space belonged to a potter. Jesse admired his work.

"You've got some cool stuff here," she said. "Do you do this for a living?"

"I do. What about you? I saw you setting up. Are you a professional, too?"

"No, it's just a hobby for me."

"Your stuff's really good."

"Thanks."

"I'm sure you'll get some good exposure here. This gig's always a fun one."

"Right on. That's good to hear. I'll talk to you later."

She walked off with a spring in her step, feeling like life was looking up. She wandered through a few more displays before returning to her section. She found Liza looking relaxed but businesslike with her Square in her phone, all set to ring up orders.

"Did you have a nice walkabout?" she asked.

"I did. Everyone is so nice and so encouraging. It's going to be a great day."

"I'm sure it is."

The show officially started at ten, but it was mostly a few stragglers for the first hour. Then, more people started to come by and really check out Jesse's work. By one, she had sold three paintings. She put more out and rearranged them for the afternoon lighting. She sold a few sketches and was feeling good as the day went on. Even people that didn't buy were very complimentary about her work. She was having a great day and was almost dreading the end of the show.

It was just after four o'clock when a dark haired woman walked up wearing a white pantsuit and large sunglasses. She reeked of class and Jesse held her breath as the woman took off her glasses to examine the paintings. Jesse couldn't help but notice the woman's stunning beauty and striking blue eyes. She couldn't resist talking to her.

"Hi there. My name's Jesse. This is my work."

"Hi, Jesse. I like your work."

"Thank you." Jesse could barely breathe. The woman was unbelievably gorgeous. She could think of nothing to say that wouldn't make her sound like an idiot, so she managed, "I'll be over here if you need anything."

The woman continued to walk through her paintings and finally walked over to Jesse. She unabashedly looked her up and down.

"Jesse, I like what I'm seeing here."

"Thank you."

"And your art's nice, too."

Jesse felt the blush and cursed herself.

"I tell you what. I want the whole lot."

"You do?"

"I do. But I want you to take me out tonight, too."

"Oh, that would be my pleasure."

Just then, Liza poked her head around from the back of the exhibit.

"Oh, I'm sorry," the woman said. "I didn't realize you were taken."

"I'm not. She's a friend who's helping me out."

The woman arched a finely shaped eyebrow at Liza.

"It's true. There's nothing between us."

"Fine. Then this lot is mine. How much do I owe you?"

Liza rang her up. The woman didn't flinch as she paid, then looked at Jesse.

"I'll meet you at seven tonight at Montoya's."

"I look forward to it," Jesse said.

"As do I."

Liza told Jesse the total amount she made as soon as the woman left.

"Holy shit! If I keep doing these shows, I might be able to retire someday," Jesse said.

"I'll say. I'd love to go out and celebrate with you, but you have other plans."

"No doubt. Wasn't she something?"

"She was indeed. A little frightening though, don't you think?"

"Not at all. A hot woman with money never frightens me. Add in good taste in art and she's just about perfect."

"Really? Do I detect some ice thawing?"

"No. I'm not ready for that. But I do think dinner and whatever follows will be most enjoyable."

"I hope so."

❖

Jesse unloaded her easels, grateful that she didn't have any art she'd had to bring home with her. She thought again of the mysterious woman and her date that night. She had to admit, she was actually a little nervous about it, but tried to shrug it off. She was just another woman, right?

She took a shower and dressed in black slacks with a white button-down shirt and a skinny black tie. She looked good and knew she'd fit in at the fancy Montoya's.

She pulled up five minutes early and walked in to find the woman in the bar, already enjoying a libation.

"And here I was sure I'd be early," Jesse said.

"I was in the neighborhood already."

"Oh. Okay. Then I won't beat myself up."

"You're not that type, are you?"

"Not so much."

"Good. I don't like weak women."

"Have you put our names in?"

"I have. Now sit and tell me about yourself."

Jesse sat down, mesmerized anew by the beautiful blue eyes staring so intently at her.

"First, why not tell me a little about you. A name, for example, would be nice."

"My name is Constance. Constance Moriarty."

"Nice to meet you Constance. How did you become a connoisseur of art?"

"We'll get to that. First you. Tell me how you got started in art. You're very good, by the way."

"Thank you. It's a hobby for me. I used to paint a lot for fun, but then shelved it for a few years and have only recently picked it back up again."

"Why did you shelve it?" Constance asked.

"I'd rather not say." Jesse didn't feel like talking about Sara at that moment.

"I think you're going to have to, if this is going to work."

Jesse felt a knot in the pit of her stomach. If what was going to work? Was Constance looking for a relationship? She wondered if she should simply excuse herself.

"Relax," Constance said. "You looked terrified. Fine. We'll come back to that. So you have a regular job and just paint for fun?"

"That's right. It's nothing serious."

They were called to their table then and Jesse breathed a sigh of relief that the inquisition was on hold at least for a few minutes.

When they were seated, Jesse quickly picked up her menu to buy some more time. She looked it over and over, even though she'd already decided what to get.

"You can't hide from me forever," Constance said.

Jesse put her menu down and smiled.

"There are just so many good choices here."

"I see."

"So what's your interest in art, Constance?"

"Truthfully, I'm an art dealer."

She reached into her purse and handed Jesse a card. Jesse simply stared at it. An art dealer? For real? She was having dinner with an art dealer. She couldn't believe her luck.

"You've got talent, Jesse. You could use some refinement, though."

"There's always room for improvement."

"Excellent answer. So, back to your break from painting. I'm interested in your work, but I need to know you're not going to just quit again. So, tell me why you quit for a few years."

Jesse took a deep breath. She swallowed hard and fought an inner battle. This was her dream, but did she feel like disclosing her pain with a total stranger?

"I lost my partner," she finally said.

"Lost as in broke up with?"

"Lost as in she died. Suddenly."

"Oh, Jesse. I'm sorry. I can understand why you lost your drive to create."

Jesse exhaled.

"But the drive is back now, and I've found someone who enjoys my work."

"Very much. I also need to know, how in love with your day job are you?"

"I'm not. But it pays the bills and then some."

"And then some, huh? So quitting it would be out of the question?"

"What are you talking about? You want me to paint full-time?"

"I want you to go to school to refine your talents. Then I want you to be a full-time artist."

Jesse sat back in the booth. Her mind was reeling at the prospect. It was more than she'd ever dreamed possible, but was it a chance she was willing to take? To turn her back on a real, established job for a chance at making a living as an artist? It didn't seem very logical to her, though part of her wanted to grab the brass ring and go for it. She didn't know what to say.

"It's okay, Jesse," Constance said. "I don't need an answer right now. But I'm very serious about this. And I'll subsidize your art school. You'll pay me back after you've had some shows and are an established artist. You think about it."

"It's just such an overwhelming prospect."

"I'm sure it is. But talent like yours doesn't come along every day. You should hone your skills and make the most of them."

CHAPTER SIX

Talk of art was tabled for the rest of dinner. Instead, they exchanged anecdotes about their childhoods and college days. Conversation was light and easy, and Jesse found herself very relaxed by the end of dinner.

"So, Jesse," Constance said after Jesse had given the waiter her credit card.

"Yes?"

"I told you this afternoon I liked what I saw. Do you remember?"

"I do." Jesse thought again of the way Constance had checked her out at the park. She felt her clit twitch.

"I still do. I assume you wouldn't be averse to taking me home tonight?"

"Not at all." Jesse was more than happy to bed Constance. She was the classiest woman she'd have in her bed in a very long time.

"We'll go to your place," Constance said.

"Are you sure? It's probably a far cry from yours."

"I don't mind. You're an artist. You could live in a loft and I wouldn't care. All I care is that you have a bed big enough for both of us."

"That I have." Jesse smiled.

"Excellent. My car's this way."

Jesse took her hand and walked with her to her Cadillac. Constance ran her fingers through Jesse's hair, causing her to shiver.

"Where are you parked?"

"I'm that truck right over there."

"I'll follow you."

Jesse was more excited with every mile. Constance was intelligent, classy, and hot. Still, she couldn't get the offer of art school out of her mind. And did Constance want a commitment? She didn't seem like it, but was she sleeping with Jesse to get her to go to art school?

Jesse told herself to relax. She was a big girl and could make her own decisions. She'd sleep with Constance, have fun, and not get sucked into anything she wasn't ready for. That decided, she relaxed and let her hormones rage at the possibility of the night ahead.

She parked her truck in her driveway, pulling in far enough to leave Constance room for her car.

"This is a nice place," Constance said as she climbed out of her car. "You made it sound like you lived in a slum or something."

"No. Just not as nice as your place."

"That's not a fair comparison to make." She took Jesse's hand. "Take me inside now."

Jesse was all revved up to take Constance to bed. And she assumed Constance was up for it, as well, but she remained cool and calm. Jesse wondered what the night ahead held. She couldn't help but wonder if Constance would let loose at all.

They walked inside and Constance stopped in the entryway to admire the paintings on the wall.

"Yes. You do have a style and quite a bit of talent," she said.

"Thank you again. Hearing that from you is high praise."

Jesse walked Constance into the living room and invited her to sit on the couch.

"I'm sorry. I don't have any wine to offer you."

"You're not much of a drinker?"

"I'm more the beer type."

"Ah, of course. No worries. Sit with me, handsome."

Jesse sat next to Constance, who immediately leaned against her. Jesse wrapped her arm around her and pulled her close. Her hair smelled of expensive fragrance and Jesse found the scent quite arousing.

"You smell amazing," she said.

"So do you. In a masculine kind of way. But I like it. There's nothing girly about you. That's so wonderful."

"Yeah? Good."

Constance shifted in her seat so she faced Jesse. She traced her jaw with her fingernails.

"Yes. You are very handsome indeed."

Jesse looked into Constance's eyes and saw the burning she'd wondered if she possessed. She lowered her mouth and caught Constance's in a soft, brief kiss. Constance's lips were tender and ready for her. The kiss sent shockwaves through Jesse's body.

"That was nice," Constance said.

"Yes, it was." Jesse kissed her again and this time Constance's mouth opened for her. She tasted sweet and Jesse forced herself not to ease her back onto the couch and take her right there. She doubted Constance was the type for sex on the couch.

When the kiss ended, Constance was breathless.

"So far, you're as talented as I'd imagined. Let's see how good you are at the rest of things." She stood. "Lead the way to the bedroom."

Jesse was happy to do just that. She was shaking with desire, her crotch wet from need. When they walked into the bedroom, Jesse moved to Constance.

"Not so fast," Constance said. "Turn the lights on. I want to see you."

Jesse was anything but shy, so she turned the lights on. It was odd to think about sex in the light, but if that's what the lady wanted, that's what the lady got.

"Any other special requests?" Jesse asked.

"Just one. Undress for me. Slowly."

Jesse untied her tie and took it off, tossing it onto the chair. She unbuttoned her shirt and took it off.

"Hold still now. Mm. You're quite a specimen, Jesse. I like what I'm seeing." She stood and stripped her own clothes off while Jesse watched. When she was naked, she leaned back on the pillows, one knee bent, the other foot on the floor. She was totally exposed to

Jesse. It took every ounce of self-control for Jesse to stand there and wait to be told what to do next.

Constance ran her fingers over her body as she lay there. Jesse struggled to remain standing on shaky knees.

"Yes, you're a fine specimen indeed." She dragged her hand between her legs, lazily stroking the area Jesse needed to have. "Go ahead and take your slacks off now. I want to see those legs."

Jesse did as she was instructed and stood on display in her boxers and undershirt.

"Oh, yes. I knew those legs would be muscular." She was rubbing her clit and Jesse couldn't take her eyes off her hand. "Turn around for me, lover. Let me see that ass."

Jesse didn't want to stop watching the show Constance was putting on, but she turned around and stood there. The room was silent, save for Constance's breathing, which was getting heavy.

"Okay, handsome, turn back around for me."

Jesse did and almost collapsed at the sight before her. Constance's fingers were inside herself, moving in and out. Jesse swallowed hard.

"Now the undershirt. Slowly. Show me your tight stomach first before I see your tits."

Jesse peeled her shirt off a little at a time, making sure to pause with the bottom of it just under her breasts.

"Oh, shit, yes," Constance said. She was rubbing all over between her legs again and Jesse wondered how she was keeping from coming. Jesse was about to cream herself and no one was touching her.

She took her shirt off and stood for inspection.

"Oh, Jesse. Look at those perfect little tits you have. They're perfect for you. Now turn around and take off your boxers so I can see that ass in the flesh."

Jesse obliged, feeling like the evidence of her arousal was running down her leg.

"Okay. Now, turn around and let me see you in all your glory."

Jesse faced Constance, who was rubbing herself frantically.

"Oh, honey, you're gorgeous. Oh yes." Her eyes closed as she leaned back. "Oh God, you're gorgeous. Oh yes. Oh God, yes."

Jesse watched in amazement as Constance brought herself to a climax.

"Come here now, dear. Clean my fingers for me."

Jesse knelt beside the bed and greedily sucked Constance's delicious fingers. They tasted salty and sweet, just as she'd known Constance would taste.

"Do you want to fuck me?" Constance asked.

Jesse could only nod.

Constance turned so she was sitting on the edge of the bed and guided Jesse's head until it was between her legs.

"Do me, Jesse."

Jesse was more than happy to follow that instruction. She buried her tongue deep inside Constance and licked every inch she could reach. She could taste her orgasm and it spurred her on, making her want to give her another and another. She ran her tongue over every inch of her then, stopping to lap at her swollen clit before licking back to her opening.

Constance had her hand on the back of Jesse's head, pressing her so hard that at times Jesse could barely breathe. Jesse was in heaven. She could stay there all night. She heard Constance breathing become labored again and licked harder and faster until Constance came again.

"Oh, yes. I knew you'd know what you were doing," Constance said.

Jesse was breathing heavily from the exertion and lack of oxygen. She climbed up onto the bed and lay on her back.

"Oh did you wear yourself out?" Constance said. She dragged her hand down Jesse's body and brought it to rest between her legs. "Oh my. Someone's a little wet."

"Imagine that," Jesse said.

"Oh, I like this. You are just perfect. Every bit of you." She slipped her fingers inside her. "You're even nice and tight. Oh, I like this."

Jesse gritted her teeth to keep from coming too soon. She didn't want to appear too easy. She was just hyper aroused and teetering on the edge. Constance was too fucking hot for words.

Constance took her fingers out and rubbed Jesse's clit.

"Does that feel good?"

"Oh yes."

"Do you want to come, Jesse?"

"I'm trying not to."

"Oh no. Don't try not to. I want to see you come. Tell me you want to come."

"I do."

"Good." She stopped what she was doing and lay down next to Jesse, who opened her eyes and looked at Constance.

"What gives?"

"Finish it, sweet one. I want to watch your face as you come. Finish it for me, please."

Jesse had no choice. She was too close not to climax. She rubbed her clit as hard as she could and closed her eyes tight. She focused on how hot Constance had looked touching herself. That's all it took for the orgasm to explode deep within her, shooting heat throughout her body.

"Oh, baby. You're gorgeous. Do you have any idea?" Constance said. She dragged her fingers over Jesse's breasts. "You're something else."

"You're rather attractive yourself," Jesse managed.

"Why thank you. I'm glad you think so." She stood and reached for her clothes. "This has been fun."

"That's it?" Jesse said.

"What did you expect?"

"I just want to make sure you're satisfied."

"Oh, Jesse. It's been a long time since I had this much fun. Thank you. But I really must get going now. Oh. And I want you to know, this has no bearing on the art school offer. This was just two women having fun, so don't feel any pressure, okay?"

"Fair enough. I'm glad to hear that."

"Walk me to the door?"

"Sure."

They got to the front door and Constance ran her fingers through Jesse's hair again.

"Thank you for tonight. It was a lot of fun."

"Thank you."

Constance kissed Jesse's cheek then disappeared into the night.

The next morning, Jesse was up bright and early. She had a lot on her mind. She didn't even know where this art school was that Constance had talked about. Not that it mattered. Quitting a good paying job to pursue her art still seemed pretty farfetched to her.

She was at work painting when Liza showed up.

"How was your night?" Liza asked.

"It was amazing. How was yours?"

"Not as fun as yours. Did you bring her home after dinner?"

"But of course." Jesse smiled.

"So who was this mystery woman?"

"Her name is Constance Moriarty and she's an art dealer."

"No shit?"

"No shit."

"And she liked your work, so?"

"So, what?"

"So what happens now?" Liza said.

"Well, to be honest, she wants me to go to art school."

"Art school on top of work? Do you have that kind of time?"

"Actually it would be art school instead of work."

"No shit?"

"Is that the phrase of the day?"

"So, what are you going to do?"

"I don't know. Part of me really wants to go for it. I mean, what an opportunity, right? But my job is really secure. I'd be a fool to give it up."

"Jesse, you hate your job. I think you'd be a fool not to go to school. Is the school here in Houston?"

"She didn't say. I assume so."

"Well, I think you should go for it."

"Why doesn't that surprise me?" Jesse said.

"Okay, I'll try to be practical. After all, how much would this school cost?"

"I don't know."

"You didn't ask?"

"She said she'd subsidize the school for me and I'd pay her back when I'm making money with my art. I'm telling you, Liza, if I wasn't such a responsible adult, I'd probably have jumped on it last night."

"Wow. Well, you certainly have a lot to think about. Are you going to see her again?"

"What do you mean?"

"I mean, will you be dating?"

"Hell, no. Nothing like that. We had fun, but that was it. I do have her card, though, and might call her to find out more about this school."

"I wish you would. If she thinks you're that good, you should go for it."

"Well, first I need to Google her and find out how legit she is."

"Right. Because stalking is the next step."

"Whatever. I don't want to quit my job for a scam artist."

"Good point."

They went into the den and Jesse searched for Constance Moriarty. They found many articles about her, some talking about art shows she put on and others extolling her philanthropic ventures.

"She looks legit," Liza said.

"Yeah, she does."

"So what do you think?"

"I think I still need to think about it."

"Well, don't think too long or the door might close. This is a chance people dream about."

"I know. Believe me, I'm aware."

Liza left and Jesse went back to her painting. The more she painted, the more she thought of Constance and her offer. She looked around her workroom and felt weird at how many pieces of art were gone. She was happy to have sold them, but it felt surreal to her. She was so used to being surrounded by her work.

She stepped away from her work in progress and fished Constance's card out of the pocket of her slacks. She stared at it for a long time before putting it under a magnet on the refrigerator door. Just in case.

❖

Work the next week was more frustrating than usual. The cliquishness of management wore on her nerves and her coworkers sucking up to them irritated her no end. If only she could do her work on her own without the petty crap that happened in the office, she'd be a happy camper. But, that wasn't the case. The work environment was part of her job and she had to accept that as long as she worked there, she'd have to put up with it. And in the back of her mind was the constant thought that she really didn't have to put up with it. She had an option now. And the longer the week dragged on, the more inviting that option looked.

By Friday night, she'd almost convinced herself to call Constance. But when she woke Saturday morning, she wasn't feeling it as strong.

Still, when Liza showed up, Jesse was sitting at her kitchen table staring at Constance's card.

"Well, this looks promising," Liza said as she handed Jesse her coffee.

"I don't know, Liza. I mean, I hate my job, but this would be such a leap of faith."

"Yes, it would, but what a leap. Call her. You deserve it."

"What if it doesn't work out?"

"What exactly did Constance say about your work? You never told me."

"She said I have a lot of talent but could use some work. You know, refine my skills and all."

"So call her. Find out about the school anyway. Do you want me to leave while you do that?"

"No, you can stay."

Jesse dialed Constance's number and was somewhat surprised it was answered on the first ring. The sound of her voice caused the butterflies in her stomach to flutter. She was really calling. She was seriously considering this.

"Constance?"

"Yes. Who's calling?"

"This is Jesse Garrett. We met last weekend?"

"Oh, Jesse," her voice was soft and sensual. "I remember you."

"Oh good. Anyway, I'm calling to find out more about this school you were telling me about."

"Really? So you're interested?"

"I think I am."

"Meet me at Bon Temps tonight at seven. We'll discuss it at length."

"I'll be there. I'll talk to you then."

"Good-bye, Jesse."

"Good-bye."

"So?" Liza said.

"So we're meeting for dinner tonight. I'll learn more there."

"Excellent. So you get laid again and get into art school. It's gonna be a good night for Jesse."

"Nobody said anything about getting laid," Jesse said. Though the thought of another night with Constance certainly appealed to her.

"Well, good for you for making that call, Jess. I'm happy for you."

"Don't go celebrating yet. Nothing's been decided." Yet, Jesse felt lighter than she had in years.

CHAPTER SEVEN

C onstance was already in the bar when Jesse arrived at the restaurant. She stood and kissed both Jesse's cheeks.

"It's nice to see you again, Jesse."

"It's good to see you, too."

"So, you're thinking seriously about art school?"

"I'm weighing my options at this point."

"Are you not much of a risk taker?"

"Not where my livelihood is concerned."

"I suppose I can't fault you there," Constance said.

They were called to their table and Jesse was beginning to wonder if even entertaining the thought of art school was a good idea. She wished she didn't have such doubt in her ability to create art.

After they'd ordered, Constance broached the subject of school again.

"So, what are your concerns? Questions? I want you to go away from dinner tonight fully armed and able to make an informed decision."

"Well, let's start with the basics. I'm assuming this school is in Houston."

Constance laughed. The sound was magical, but unnerving at the same time.

"What's so funny?"

"Oh, Jesse. I want you to have the very best instruction you can. I don't know that you'd get that here. I'm sure there are good art schools here, but I want you to have the best. The school I'd send you to is in Paris."

"Paris? As in France?" Jesse could hardly believe her ears.

"Yes, dear. As in France."

Jesse sat back against the booth.

"Oh, wow. I didn't see that coming."

"Have you ever been?"

"No. I don't get to Europe much." Jesse was sorry for the sarcasm as soon as it was out.

"Well, everyone should go at least once."

"I don't know that I'd learn much there. I don't speak a word of French. Heck, I have a hard enough time with the English language."

Constance laughed again.

"You do fine with English. And you needn't worry about French. I'll be sending you to a place where they offer classes in English, as well."

Jesse nodded her understanding, her mind still wrestling with the concept.

"And I will pay for your way there and your lodging, as well as your education. Incidentals will be up to you."

"How long would I be there?"

"A year."

"A year? That's a long time to be away."

"From what, Jesse? You won't have a job to worry about. You have no partner, no pets that I saw. What's to keep you here?"

Jesse pondered the question. What was there to keep her in the States? Her family lived in California and she only saw them every year or so as it was. There was Liza, of course, but she knew Liza would never let her use her as an excuse not to go. There was her house. She'd have to figure out what to do about that. She supposed she could rent it out for a year.

"I see those wheels turning," Constance said. "What are you thinking?"

"I don't know. It's such a huge leap of faith. I just don't know."

"Jesse, I'm an art dealer. I know good art when I see it. I wouldn't begin to make this kind of an investment if I didn't feel you have what it takes to give me a good return on that investment."

"Still. A year in Paris."

"Some people would kill for this chance."

"I know."

"Well, you can still think about it, if you need to."

Jesse finally recognized the implication of it all. The fog lifted and she allowed herself to absorb what was actually happening. She had the opportunity to quit her dead-end job and never see those annoying people again. She could go to Paris for a year. Paris! And she could paint for a living. She could spend her life doing what she really loved, what she was truly passionate about.

"Screw it," Jesse said. "I'll do it."

"You will?" Constance seemed genuinely surprised. "That's great news! You won't be sorry, Jesse. I promise."

"So, let's work out the details. When do I leave? How do I register? There's so much to think about."

"Don't you worry about registration or anything of the like. I think their classes start around May first for this term. So you'll have a couple of weeks." She hailed the waiter. "Bring us some Dom Pérignon."

"Wow. That's pricey."

"Don't worry. This meal is on me. I'm thrilled you're doing this. I'd hate to see a talent like yours wasted."

"You really do believe in me, don't you?"

"I really do. And I'm happy to see you're starting to believe in you, too. And believe in me, for that matter. I won't steer you wrong."

"For some reason, I believe you."

"Good."

They ate and drank and Jesse was sorry to see the evening come to an end. After Constance paid their tab, she turned to Jesse.

"I don't know about you, but I'd like to keep the celebration going."

"What do you have in mind?"

"You."

"Me, huh?"

"Yes, you. I'll follow you back to your place again."

"That would be wonderful."

This time, as soon as they got in the house, Constance was in Jesse's arms. Jesse kissed her passionately and swooned as the kiss was returned in kind.

"Take me to your room, Jesse. I need you now."

Jesse was happy to oblige. She turned on all the lights and pulled Constance to her again.

"What kinds of games are in store for me this time?" Jesse asked.

"None. You're going to make love to me until I'm exhausted.

"Sounds good to me."

Jesse helped Constance out of her clothes and laid them carefully on the chair. Jesse stared in amazement at the beauty that was Constance. She stripped quickly out of her own clothes and lay on the bed, pulling Constance with her.

They kissed again as their limbs entwined. Jesse rubbed her legs over Constance's, loving the silky smooth feeling of her skin. Constance ran her hands over Jesse's back and Jesse loved the feel of her fingernails lightly scratching her. Every inch that Constance touched came alive with desire.

"You feel amazing," Jesse said.

Constance pried Jesse's legs open and slid her hand between them.

"Oh, Jesse. You feel very good, too."

Jesse lay on her back and spread her legs wider, inviting Constance to do what she would.

Constance ran her fingernails over Jesse's swollen clit, eliciting groans from Jesse. Jesse couldn't believe the sensations she was feeling. Every stroke pushed her onward, every touch made her crave more.

Jesse grabbed hold of the sheets when Constance finally delved inside her. She filled her completely and Jesse arched her back, meeting each of Constance's thrusts. She needed more and Constance gave it to her.

Jesse cried out as the orgasms tore through her body, one after another. She lost count of how many times she came.

"Oh, dear God. How did you do that?" Jesse managed when she finally caught her breath.

"Oh, Jesse. You were made to please. I suppose you spend so much time pleasing others that you don't allow yourself the pleasure you deserve. You need to be loved more often."

"And speaking of pleasure. I believe it's your turn now."

Constance started to object.

"I'm fine. I should probably get going."

"No way. You look too good for me not to enjoy."

Constance rolled over to her back and Jesse once again took in how beautiful she was.

"I want all of you. I don't even know where to start," Jesse said.

"I'm sure you'll figure it out."

Jesse ran her hand the length of Constance's body, bringing her hand to rest on one of Constance's breasts. She smiled at the instant response she created. Constance's nipple hardened and puckered.

Jesse replaced her hand with her mouth. She licked her nipple all over before sucking it deep in her mouth.

"Oh yes," Constance said.

Jesse continued to suck harder while Constance tangled her fingers in Jesse's hair. Jesse released her grip on the nipple and kissed down Constance's trim belly. Constance spread her legs and Jesse climbed between them.

She kissed Constance's clit, enjoying anew the taste of her. She flicked her tongue over it before moving lower to run her tongue over her opening. She buried it deep inside her, greedily devouring her. She tasted sweet and tangy and Jesse couldn't get enough of her.

"My clit, Jesse. Please."

Jesse was happy to oblige. She sucked Constance's clit, rolling her tongue over it.

"Oh yes. That's it. Oh yes."

Jesse continued to play with her. She felt Constance tense up and knew she was close. She finally cried out as her body shuttered when she reached her climax.

They lay together with Jesse holding Constance.

"That was nice," Constance said.

"Yeah, it was."

Constance propped herself up on an elbow.

"You know, Jesse, I'm really happy you're going to school."

"Thanks. I really appreciate the opportunity."

"You're going to be so happy. Your life is about to change drastically."

"Yeah, it is."

"But it'll be all for the better, believe me."

"I have to believe you. I'm putting all my trust in you right now. That's not normal for me."

"I realize that. But I won't steer you wrong."

"I hope not. I'm still scared. But I guess I've made up my mind and need to just relax and go with it."

"Yes, you do. You need to relax and know that soon you'll be making your living through your art. What a rewarding way to live, right?"

"Exactly."

"Good. And now, it's time for me to get going. This has been fun. And I'll be in touch with you about the school."

"Don't you need my number for that?"

"Oh, yes. I'll get that before I leave. And we'll meet again to get all the forms filled out and things settled."

"Sounds good."

Constance got up and quickly dressed. She handed her phone to Jesse.

"Enter your number for me."

Jesse did as she was asked.

"So, when should I expect to hear from you?"

"Maybe next weekend we'll plan to get together."

"That sounds good." Jesse was wondering if they'd end up in bed together again.

"Now show me out," Constance said.

Jesse pulled on her boxers and undershirt and walked Constance to the door.

"Tonight was fun," she said.

"It was. But don't get used to it. I might find you attractive, but your education is my main goal. I'm not looking for anything else from you. I want you to be a successful artist. You're my investment, not my lover."

"Understood. But the sex is good."

"Yes, it is." Constance laughed. "It really is."

"Okay, well, I look forward to hearing from you."

"You will. Good night, Jesse."

"Good night."

Jesse fell into a deep sleep and awoke feeling conflicted. Part of her was excited, yet she was still scared. She hoped she wasn't making the mistake of a lifetime. Sure, if after a year in Paris, she didn't make it as an artist, she could try to find a new job. But she wasn't getting any younger and how hard would it be to find a new job? And would she be able to live off an entry-level income?

She tried to shake the fears from her mind. She needed to focus on the possibility that she would be a successful artist. She would make it her livelihood. She would be happy. She tried very hard to convince herself.

She was in her workroom when Liza showed up with her Sunday morning coffee.

"How was your night?" Liza asked.

"It was great."

"Yeah? Did she come home with you again?"

"She did."

"Oh my. That's a repeat for you. Am I hearing wedding bells?"

"Not even close," Jesse said.

"That's too bad. She's successful, attractive and she believes in you. Sounds like a winner to me."

"She's not looking for that. And neither am I."

"Fine. So, how was dinner? What did we learn? And where's this art school?"

"Dinner was great. And, well, that art school? Yeah. It's in Paris," Jesse said.

"Paris? I'm guessing that's not Paris, Texas?"

"You're correct."

"Seriously? So it's in Paris, Paris?"

"Yes. Seriously. It's in Paris, France."

"So, what does that mean?" Liza asked.

"What do you mean?"

"I mean, what do you think? Talk to me."

"Well, to be honest, it hit me last night that I'd be a fool to pass up an opportunity for a year in Paris."

"A *year*?"

"Yep. And she's paying for everything. The school, my room and board, my way to and from there. I just have to pay for my entertainment needs."

"Wait. You make it sound like it's a done deal."

"It is. School starts in May," Jesse said.

Liza sat down at the table. Jesse joined her.

"What are you thinking?" Jesse asked.

"I'm just trying to absorb everything."

"I thought you'd be happy for me."

"I am. Oh, don't get me wrong. I'm very happy for you. It's just all happening so fast."

"I know, right?"

"I can't believe you're walking away from that horrible place you work finally. That's gotta feel like a major relief," Liza said.

"It feels like a huge weight has been lifted off my shoulders. I'm going to walk in tomorrow and give my two week's notice. Can you imagine how good that's going to feel?"

"That's awesome."

Liza stood and hugged Jesse.

"I'm so happy for you."

"Thanks. I still can't believe I'm doing this. Part of me still thinks I must be crazy."

"Nah. You'd be crazy not to be doing this."

"I do have a favor to ask of you."

"What's that?"

"Will you play landlord for me? I'm not going to have time to get my house rented out for the year, but I was hoping you'd take care of it. I really don't want to leave it empty."

"No worries," Liza said. "I'd be happy to do that for you. I'll find responsible tenants and do all that landlord-type stuff."

"Great. Thanks. That's a relief."

"So what kinds of classes will you be taking?"

"I don't know. We're going to talk more next week."

"Oh, my. So another date?"

"I guess. But it's all about school."

"Sure," Liza said. "Just like last night was."

Jesse blushed.

"Well, dinner was all about school. The champagne we drank might have lowered our inhibitions a bit."

"Yeah, like you need champagne to lower your inhibitions."

"Guilty. And she's so fucking hot. I mean, she is one attractive woman."

"Are you sure she knows she's not a long term thing for you? I'd hate for that to put the kibosh on this school thing."

"No. She made it clear that she doesn't want anything like that from me."

"Good. Maybe you'll meet some hot mademoiselle who'll knock you for a loop."

"I wouldn't count on it," Jesse said.

"No, I guess you wouldn't."

CHAPTER EIGHT

Jesse walked in to the human resource department with her letter in hand the very next day. Her stomach was full of butterflies as the reality of what she was doing continued to sink in with each passing moment. Still, she waited in the waiting area, determined not to chicken out.

She was finally called in.

"Well, hello, Jesse. This is a rare treat," the human resource specialist said.

"How you doing?"

"I'm fine. To what do I owe this visit?"

Jesse balked. She still had time to walk away. Nothing was set in motion yet. She could change her mind and life could go on.

"Um, I need to talk to you."

"I gathered that. What's going on?"

Jesse handed her the envelope that held her letter to the company.

"I'm um, actually, um…I'm giving my two weeks notice."

"You are?" She took the envelope and set it to the side. "This is very unexpected."

"I realize that. But it's something I have to do."

"Have you found another job elsewhere?"

"Not exactly."

"Jesse, you've been here a long time. If it's more money you need, I can check with accounting and see if there's any way we can give you a raise."

"No, ma'am. That's not it." Though it would have been nice to know that could have been an option in the past, Jesse thought.

"Has something happened? Do you want to talk about it? Did one of your coworkers do something? Feel free to speak freely to me, Jesse."

"No, no. It's nothing like that. I promise." The thought crossed her mind to take the opportunity to talk about how cliquey and unprofessional management was, but she reasoned there was no point in that.

"I just have an opportunity that is too good to pass up."

"So it *is* another job."

"No. I'll be going back to school." Jesse didn't want to go into the whole thing with this woman. Besides, she knew how foolish she'd sound saying she was quitting her job to pursue a life as an artist. And the company didn't need to know. She just wanted to get out of there.

"Well, maybe you can work part-time. I'm sure we could work something out with you."

Jesus Christ, Jesse thought. How hard was it to quit?

"No, thank you. I appreciate the offer, but I'll be moving out of the area for school."

She stood, hoping the woman would take the hint.

"Well, Jesse, if you're serious, I suppose I have no choice but to accept your letter of resignation. Though I must tell you, you've always been such a good worker. We'll be very sorry to see you go."

"I'm sorry to leave," Jesse heard herself say. "But it's what I need to do."

"Well, we wish you the best in all your future endeavors."

"Thank you."

Jesse walked out of the room on shaky legs. She'd done it. She'd actually done it.

She stepped outside and called Liza.

"I did it," she said.

"With whom?" Liza answered.

"Very funny. I mean I gave my notice."

"Most excellent! Good for you, Jess. That has to feel amazing."

"It does. Oh my God, you wouldn't believe how hard she tried to convince me to stay."

"Are you kidding me?"

"I am not. It was like I'd stepped in quicksand and was never going to get out. It was horrible. But I stuck to my guns and did it."

"Very cool. We'll go out tonight to celebrate. Meet me at The Black Hole after work."

"Will do. Okay, I still need to work for the next two weeks, so I guess I'd better get back inside."

"Okay. I'll see you tonight."

Jesse met Liza after work, where Liza already had tequila shots and Coronas ordered for them.

"We need to be able to drive home tonight," Jesse said.

"No worries. We won't overdo it. I was going to order champagne, but thought it probably wouldn't measure up to whatever Constance ordered."

"Try Dom Pérignon."

"No shit?"

"Nothing but the best for me." Jesse laughed.

"I guess. So, wow. You're really doing this. You quit your job. That's fucking awesome."

"Tell me."

"Do you know where you'll live or anything yet?"

"Nope. All I did Saturday was agree to it. She said she'd take care of everything and I guess I was too excited to ask for details."

"I'm so proud of you, Jess. To your future." She held up her shot glass.

"To being a world renowned artist." Jesse clinked glasses with Liza and they both downed their tequila.

"Can you even imagine?" Liza said.

"Not really." Jesse laughed. "I think I just need to get through school and have a few shows before the reality of what might be becomes tangible to me."

"I'm sure. Well, I can imagine it. I'll be saying I knew you when."

"You'll be with me every step of the way."

"Yeah, except that year you're in Paris."

"You can come visit."

"Yeah. Maybe I will."

"Maybe? I'm counting on it," Jesse said.

"I'll start saving now."

"You'd better."

They finished their beers and had another round.

"No more nine-to-five grind," Liza said. "I'm so jealous."

"You should be. I'll be in a foreign land where everyone speaks a language I don't understand trying to refine my skills to pursue a dream. Yeah. That sounds better."

"You're pursuing a dream." Liza laughed. "The rest? Hell, you'll figure it out. Besides, everyone speaks the language of love, so I'm sure you'll make out just fine."

"I hope so. I sure don't plan on taking any vow of celibacy while I'm over there."

"I don't think anyone would expect that of you. Except Constance, but you keep saying it's not like that with her."

"It's not. I'm not worried about her," Jesse said.

"Will she be flying to Paris to check on you?"

"I don't know. Somehow I doubt it. I get the feeling she keeps herself pretty busy."

"Good. I don't want you to have a stalker."

"Not even a rich, gorgeous one?"

"Not even."

Jesse laughed.

"No. No worries there. I promise."

"Good. And thank God for e-mail so you can keep me informed on all your escapades."

"You know it."

"And maybe you'll find a lesbian bar over there so you can continue your streak of meaningless one-night stands," Liza said.

"One can only hope."

They finished their second round and Liza ordered a third.

"No more after this. We really do have to drive," Jesse said.

"Fine. But this is a celebration."

"Yes, it is."

They did their shots of tequila when Jesse's phone rang. She saw it was Constance and excused herself to take the call. Once outside where she could hear, she answered.

"Hello?"

"Hello, Jesse?"

"Yes."

"It's Constance."

"Hi."

"I need some information from you to get you registered for classes. Can you meet me for dinner tomorrow night?"

"Sure. Where?"

"La Mirage. Say six o'clock?"

"I'll be there."

She walked back in to the bar.

"What's up?" Liza asked.

"I'm meeting Constance at La Mirage tomorrow night to go over registration stuff."

"Cool. And I guess it won't matter if you're late to work the next day, what with you quitting and all."

"Why would I be late?" Jesse asked.

"I'm guessing it'll be a late night for you."

"I doubt that."

"I'm betting on it."

Jesse couldn't suppress a grin. She was hoping to have another night with Constance before it really became all business, but she wasn't counting on it.

"Yeah, look at you. You are betting on it, too."

"Nope. Hoping? Sure. Betting? Not so much."

"Okay, well, let's finish these beers and get going. Thanks for letting me take you out to celebrate."

"Thank you. This has been fun."

"Yeah, it has. Man, I hate to be a Debbie Downer, but I'm sure gonna miss you when you're gone."

"It's only for a year. And we'll keep in touch."

"Yeah, we will."

They finished their beers and Jesse drove home. She climbed into bed, but sleep escaped her. She tossed and turned, more excited by the minute about the prospect of her new life.

She woke in the morning, tired, but excited. She thought about calling in sick to work to spend the day working on her paintings, but knew that wouldn't be the responsible thing to do.

Jesse made it through the day, working on new policies and helping with claim reports. She didn't know how she was able to focus, but she was. The workday finally ended and she drove home to change for dinner.

She found herself looking forward to dinner with Constance as much to talk about school as seeing Constance. That surprised her, but now that she'd taken the first step, she was anxious to make the rest happen.

Constance was already at a table when Jesse arrived. She stood and kissed Jesse on both cheeks.

"I'm so glad you could meet me on such short notice."

"My pleasure. What do you need from me?"

Constance laughed.

"My, aren't we excited to get started."

"I'm sorry. It's just that I really am excited."

"Well, let's order dinner first and then we'll talk business."

They ordered, though Jesse could barely sit still in her excitement. When the waiter had taken their menus, Constance got out her tablet.

"I just need to ask a few questions. I don't know much about you and they need basic information for registration."

"Like what?"

"Like your birthday."

"November twelve, nineteen seventy-three."

"And your address."

They went through basic questions and finally Constance announced the form was complete just as dinner was served. They talked as they ate.

"You'll be staying in the dormitory there," Constance said.

"Aren't I a little old for the dorms?" Jesse asked. "When I was in school, the dorms were filled with partying kids and loud music. I'm not so much into that scene anymore."

"The dorms there aren't like that. They are filled with serious students such as yourself."

"Okay. If you say so."

"I do. And don't worry. You'll have your own room. The dorms are much different. They're basically apartments. You'll spend most of your time at school, either in class or in a drawing or painting room. You're going to love it."

"Again. I have to trust you."

"Yes, you do."

"So now that you're registered, we just need to get you there. Oh, Jesse. I'm so happy for you."

"Me, too. I can hardly think of anything else."

"Great. That's what I want to hear. Now, when can you fly out?"

"I gave my notice at work. So my last day will be a week from Friday. So basically any time after that."

"Sounds good. We'll give you a week to get everything together and fly you out the following weekend. You'll have a few days before school starts to look around and get acclimated."

Jesse was suddenly nervous. Where would she go? Who would she get in touch with? She almost wished Constance was going with her to ease her into her new life. She told herself she was being ridiculous. She was an adult. A very independent one, at that. She'd be fine.

"What are you thinking?" Constance asked.

"I was just kind of overwhelmed at the thought of going there, not knowing where I'm going or what I'm doing. But I guess I'll figure it all out, won't I?"

"We'll get you to Paris. You'll get a taxi to the university. From there, you'll figure out where you need to go and how to get there. Paris is a gem. You'll want to explore every inch of it, believe me. And you'll get there a few days early to check it out. But don't overdo it. I want you to be fresh and ready when school starts."

"I won't go crazy. I'll just see the sights and get acclimated. I'll save the partying until I know what I'm in for."

"There's just so much to see. I'm jealous. I haven't been back in several years. Maybe I'll come visit you some time this year."

"That would be great."

After dinner, they went back to Jesse's house.

"You understand that there's no commitment between us, right?" Constance said as she undressed.

"I do. I hope you do, too."

"I do. I don't want you to think I'm going to pine for you or anything while you're gone."

"I don't. We're just having fun."

"Yes, we are." Constance pushed Jesse on the bed and straddled her. She fondled her breasts as she ground into Jesse's belly.

"You are so hot," Jesse said. She slid her hand between them and found Constance's wet clit ready for her. She pinched it between her fingers and pressed into it. She watched Constance's face contort in pleasure. She moved lower and plunged her fingers deep inside her.

Constance placed her hands on either side of Jesse's head and bobbed up and down on her fingers. She gyrated on them as Jesse kept her gaze on her face. She saw Constance bite her lip and close her eyes and she knew she was close.

Constance suddenly rolled off Jesse.

"What?" Jesse asked.

"I need your mouth on me."

Jesse climbed between her legs. She moved her fingers back inside while she licked and sucked on her clit.

"Yes, Jesse. Yes. That's it."

Jesse needed no further encouragement. She was loving what she was doing and was soon rewarded as Constance screamed out as the orgasms crashed over her.

"Oh, Jesse. You are indeed a talented lover."

Jesse said nothing as she continued to lick Constance's clit ever so lightly.

"Come up here and lay with me."

Jesse lay next to Constance, who once again dragged her hand all over Jesse's body.

"I love your body, Jesse."

"Thank you. I love yours."

"We're good together. That's for sure. In bed and out."

Jesse's stomach tightened. What happened to all that talk about no commitment?

"Um…I thought you said there was nothing between us outside of bed," she said.

"Oh I don't mean that way. I mean in terms of your art and my ability to help make you better and promote you. Don't worry. I meant what I said."

"Oh, good. And I hope I don't let you down with my art."

"You won't. I just need you to sign my contract. I forgot to have you do that. It will give me the rights to your first five shows."

Jesse sat up.

"You mean you get all the profits from my shows?"

"Not all of them, of course. But I get to stage them and will take a percentage of sales. You can't go through another dealer."

"Oh." Jesse lay back down. "That makes sense. I wouldn't have dreamed of doing that."

"Right now you say that. But things happen over the course of a year. I'll have that contract just in case you think about changing your mind."

"That sounds fair."

"I think so. Now, where were we?"

She kissed Jesse, who immediately lost all thought of art school and shows. She could focus only on the kiss and the response her body had.

She was swollen and wet and ready when Constance finally touched her. She came almost instantly.

"Damn, what you do to me."

"You were easy tonight."

"I was ready for you."

"Apparently." Constance laughed softly. "Oh, Jesse. I do hope Paris will be ready for you."

"I hope I'm ready for Paris."

"You are, Jesse. Indeed you are."

CHAPTER NINE

Jesse's plane touched down at Charles du Galle airport on a rainy evening. She gathered her bags and hailed a taxi. She gave the driver the address for the *Académie de Beauté*. The driver entered the address in her GPS and Jesse was off. She looked at the buildings they passed and felt like a stranger in a strange land. Of course, she was. She definitely wasn't in Houston anymore.

The architecture amazed her. It was so European. It was exactly as she'd always imagined it. It was beautiful. She couldn't wait to paint the buildings. In her mind's eye, she could see the streets teeming with people. She wanted to paint those scenes, as well. She hoped for some nice weather in the coming days so she could watch the city come alive.

They arrived at the dormitory and she took in the beautiful building she would call home for the next year. It was Baroque style and three stories tall. She grabbed her things and walked to the front door. She swiped the card Constance had given her just before she left. The doors unlocked and she walked in. The inside was fairly nondescript. There was a desk there that was empty at the moment. The rest were just doors and stairs and a bank of elevators. She took the elevator to the second floor and found her apartment. Number 269. She smiled again at the number and let herself in.

The apartment was tiny, but nicely furnished. And Constance was right; she wouldn't be spending a lot of time there. There was a living room with a couch, a desk and a television; a very small kitchen with the basics; and a bedroom with a closet, a bed, two nightstands and lamps. There was also a closet with a washer and dryer in it. It was cozy and Jesse went to work unpacking.

When she had everything put away, she realized she was hungry. She couldn't remember the last time she'd eaten. She wondered where she could find food and decided there was no time like the present to check out the neighborhood. Constance had told her it was a very safe area, so she wasn't worried about wandering alone.

She stepped out into the night rain and looked up and down the street. There was a café just a block south of her, so she walked there to get dinner.

It was called *Café de L'artiste*, which sounded promising to her. The place was fairly busy, even at eight o'clock. She found a table and picked up a menu, half afraid she wouldn't understand it. It was written in both English and French, though, which made her more comfortable. Although she realized she could easily have recognized a burger and fries in French.

The waitress came over and asked if she wanted anything to drink. Her accent was thick and it took a couple of tries before Jesse understood her. She looked at the beer list and didn't recognize any of the offerings. She ordered a Kronenbourg and hoped for the best. She wondered how long it would take her to get used to the accent of the country. She knew she'd hear it all the time and hated having to ask people to repeat what they said.

When the waitress brought her beer, Jesse ordered her dinner and sat back, suddenly exhausted. She'd eat dinner then get to the apartment and sleep, so she'd be able to get up early and explore the city the next day.

Dinner was brought to her by a different woman. This woman was almost as tall as Jesse, with gray hair and bright green eyes. She was stunning and Jesse's mouth went dry when she spoke in a lilting French accent.

"You're new here, aren't you?" the woman asked.

"I am. I just got here today."

"Are you an art student?"

"I am," Jesse said again. She felt stupid for repeating herself.

"My name is Odette," the woman said. "This is my café. I wanted to introduce myself to you. This place is popular with the students. I hope we'll see a lot of you."

Jesse struggled for something to say. She wanted to keep talking to Odette, to keep hearing her soft, melodic voice.

"So far, so good," she said. "It's a very comfortable place you have."

"*Oui*. We try to keep it that way. And it's very close to school, so it's convenient, no?"

"It's very convenient. And you have good beer." Jesse held up her empty bottle as proof.

"I'll have Giselle bring you a refill. But if you just got here today, you must be exhausted. Don't overdo the beer or you'll pass out at your table. That's not a very good first impression." She laughed.

Jesse laughed with her.

"No, I won't be doing that."

"I will let you eat now. If you ever need anything, you just ask for Odette and I'll make sure you're taken care of."

"Thank you. I really appreciate that."

Odette winked at her then turned and walked off. A moment later, Giselle appeared with another beer. Jesse thanked her and dug into her dinner.

She was happy and tired when she left the diner. The walk in the rain did nothing to wake her up. She got home and fell into a happy sleep, with visions of Odette dancing in her head.

The next morning dawned gray but dry. Jesse went to the desk on the first floor and got a schedule and map for the Metro. She found the nearest station and took the subway to the Champs Elysees. This was the Paris she wanted to see. She would go to the Arc de Triomphe, and Notre Dame and the Louvre eventually. She had to since she was in Paris. But this street was where Paris's heart beat.

As she walked the street, she saw several artists with their easels, each doing their best to capture the Paris spirit. Her heart raced at the thought that she would soon be one of them. She was excited at the prospect. She walked past all the high-end stores and stopped to gaze in them, looking less at the merchandise and more at the shoppers. They were dressed very nicely and held themselves with an air that was truly Parisian. Jesse was in heaven. She would come alive in this new city. Her opportunities abounded.

After spending several hours people watching, she walked farther down the street to the Arc de Triomphe. She was in awe of its power and beauty. She took several pictures, hoping they would do it justice as she was determined to sketch it that night.

Jesse knew she'd come back, but was still anxious to see more of the city. Paris seemed surreal to her. It was hard to believe she was really there, experiencing all of it.

Tired and hungry, she caught the Metro back to the station closest to her school. She walked over to the café for dinner and hoped Odette would come talk to her again. She was fortunate to get there when things were slow. Odette greeted her at the door.

"My American stranger. You're back. You must have enjoyed your dinner last night?"

"Very much," Jesse said.

"You know, you didn't tell me your name. If we're to be friends, shouldn't I know that?"

Jesse hoped they would be more than friends eventually, at least for a night.

"My name is Jesse."

"Jesse. How wonderfully American."

"Yes. I suppose it is."

"Tell me, Jesse. How did you spend your first full day in Paris?"

"I went to the Champs Elysees and the Arc de Triomphe."

"Oh, wonderful. There's so much to see here."

"Yes, there is. It's an artist's dream."

"Do you need any tips or anything? I will be happy to tell you anything I know."

"Actually, I will eventually need groceries. Is there a market nearby?"

"There is a market just three blocks north of here. But I prefer the *marché* two blocks south."

"What's the difference?" Jesse asked.

"The one two blocks south is open air. You know? The bread is fresh daily. The fruits and vegetables handpicked."

"Oh, that sounds much more my speed."

"*Oui*? You like that?"

"Yes. Yes, I do. I'll go there tomorrow," Jesse said. "Is there meat there?"

"*Oui*. There is a butcher who is there some days. I do not know if he'll be there tomorrow."

"Well, I'll check it out."

"Good. Now sit. I'll bring you a beer. What do you want for dinner?"

"I think I'd like to try something more French than a burger and fries tonight."

Odette laughed. It was music to Jesse's ears.

"You look at the menu. I'll bring your beer and take your order."

Jesse looked around. There were waitresses caring for other patrons. She didn't know how she'd lucked out to get Odette. Maybe she was just the local Welcome Wagon for new students. It didn't matter. Jesse knew she'd have to start cooking for herself, but it was nice to know this café was there for when she didn't feel like it.

Odette was back.

"Have you decided on dinner?"

"I'm sorry. I haven't looked at the menu yet."

"Fine. I will bring you our special. It is bacon and leek quiche. You'll love it."

"Sounds delicious." Jesse put her menu down and mustered her courage. "Do you ever take breaks?"

"Oh, Jesse. This is my life and my love. I don't need breaks. Now you relax. Dinner will be here soon."

Jesse exhaled. She just wanted Odette to sit with her and talk to her. But she did have a business to run and Jesse understood that. She enjoyed her beer and Odette brought her another before she could ask. She was halfway through it when Odette arrived with her quiche.

The quiche was delicious. It melted in her mouth. The cheese was different than she was used to and when Odette came to check on her, she asked what it was.

"It's Gruyere," she said, her accent playing over the word.

"I'm not going to try to say that," Jesse laughed. "But it's delicious."

She finished her dinner, paid her tab, and walked to the apartment. She needed to think of it as home, but she wasn't quite there yet. She walked in and grabbed a sketchpad from her closet. She set it up in the living room and pulled her picture of the Arc de Triomphe up on her phone. She propped up her phone and began to sketch. She was exhausted by the time she was finished, but she was happy with the end result. She'd buy a frame and put it on her wall. It was the first piece of art she'd created in her new life and she wanted it displayed.

She woke the next morning late and decided to visit the open air market Odette had told her about. She heard the people before she got there, their voices a mingle of different languages. She thought she could make out English, but it was really a cacophony she heard.

She browsed the stalls and bought some fresh baguettes and vegetables. She was in luck that the butcher was there so she was able to get some meat for the next few days. As she walked by a florist, she heard her call out.

"*Madame? Voulez-vous des fleurs pour votre amie?*"

Jesse turned and saw the woman motioning to her.

"I'm sorry," Jesse said. "I don't understand."

"Ah. No French?"

"No. Only English."

"Okay. Would you like flowers for your girlfriend?"

"I don't have a girlfriend."

"A woman as, how do you say, handsome as you?"

Jesse laughed. The woman was beautiful, with long dark hair and amber eyes. Jesse was amused at the exchange.

"Thank you, but no. I have no girlfriend."

"You have been in Paris long?"

"No. Just a couple of days."

"Soon then. Some lucky lady will snatch you up. Paris is the city of love."

Jesse thought it was the City of Lights, but she wasn't about to argue with this beauty. She laughed again.

"I think I'll be too busy with school for that," Jesse said.

"You go to the *Académie* then?"

"Yes. Or I will. This term."

"You need someone to show you around the city." It wasn't a question.

"I did some sightseeing yesterday. And I'll do some more today."

"Ah, but Paris has such a nightlife. I will show you. Meet me here at seven. I will take you to dinner and to a club. We'll have fun."

Jesse wasn't about to turn down an offer from such a beautiful woman.

"I'd like that."

"Bring money for taxi and drinks."

Jesse laughed. She liked a woman who was straightforward.

"I will."

"I must get back to work. I will see you at seven."

Jesse took her groceries home and put them away before embarking on another expedition into the city. This time, her destination was Notre Dame. She packed a sketchpad and headed out. When she arrived, she was blown away at the beauty of the cathedral. Sure, she had seen pictures of it, but none did justice to the beautiful French Gothic architecture. She was amazed at the sheer magnitude of the building. She even fell in love with the gargoyles perched atop it.

She sketched for a while, trying to capture its eminence before she put her sketchpad away and went inside. The vaulted ceilings and stained glass windows took her breath away. She was mesmerized by all she saw. She walked the length of the building and sat in the first pew, taking in the majestic altar. The statues there were so finely sculpted. The place was an art lover's dream. She finally let herself out and made her way back to her apartment where she showered and dressed for her evening on the town.

She wore gray slacks and a purple golf shirt. She looked nice enough to be comfortable wherever they went. She knew she'd feel neither over- nor underdressed. She slipped on her loafers and walked down the street to where the stalls were all boarded up for the night. She checked her watch. She still had five minutes. She had nothing to do but wait.

At seven fifteen, she was about to head home when the flower saleswoman walked up wearing a long paisley skirt and a white peasant's top.

"In Paris, time is suggested," she said. "So I'm not really late. You'll learn this."

Jesse had to smile. She didn't know whether to believe her or not. She supposed it could be true.

Jesse extended her hand.

"I'm Jesse."

"My name is Amelie."

"That's a pretty name."

"It's, how do you say, common here."

"Really?"

"Yes. But thank you."

"So where to, Amelie?"

"We are going to the Champs Elysees. There is a restaurant there you have to try. I will pay. Then to a club."

"Sounds good."

They walked up the block past the university to a main street and hailed a taxi.

"Martinique's," Amelie told the driver.

He zoomed through town, zigging and zagging through traffic. Jesse wondered if this was what it felt like to be in a taxi in New York. She was almost nauseous when he pulled up in front of a white façade with no marking.

"You will pay him," Amelie said.

Jesse smiled and paid the cabbie. Amelie took her hand and led her down an alley and into the side door of a small restaurant. There were only twenty tables, most of which were full.

"Amelie!" The maître d' shouted as he gave her a hug and kissed both her cheeks.

"This is a friend from America," she said.

He hugged Jesse and kissed her cheeks as well.

"Welcome, American friend. Come." He led them to a table and handed them two menus.

The place was decorated in ocean décor, with seascapes on the wall and fishnets hanging from the ceiling. It smelled amazing, the air carrying scents of spices Jesse didn't recognize. Her stomach growled loudly as she realized she hadn't eaten at all that day.

"You are hungry," Amelie said.

"I am."

"I will order for us."

While Jesse liked Amelie's attitude, her butch feathers got a little ruffled. Until she looked at the menu and realized she didn't understand a word of it.

"That would be wonderful," she said.

"Do like red or white wine?"

"Red, please."

"Very good."

Amelie ordered and soon the waiter brought a bottle of Bordeaux. He handed the cork to Jesse. It smelled fine. He poured a little in her glass. She sipped it and nodded to him. He filled Amelie's glass and then hers.

"This is very good," Jesse said.

"Yes. I knew you would like."

"Very much."

Dinner was served with dishes Jesse could not pronounce. Nor did she know what they contained, but she enjoyed every delicious bite.

"This restaurant is very good, yes?"

"Yes, indeed," Jesse said. "It's amazing."

When they finished dinner, Jesse asked what was next on the agenda.

"Next we go dance."

Jesse was looking forward to watching Amelie's body sway and gyrate to music.

"What club are we going to?"

"It is, how you say, women's club. It's just up the street."

"That sounds great to me."

"It costs nothing to get in."

"That sounds even better," Jesse said.

They walked into the night and Amelie took Jesse's hand.

"You like Paris?" she asked.

"I do."

"You like me?"

"I do."

"Good. I like you, too."

CHAPTER TEN

Amelie led them down the street and Jesse could hear music wafting out of the establishment long before they reached it. The beat pulsated on the night air. The night was looking promising, to be sure.

The building had dark windows in the front, but the door was open. They walked in and Amelie was greeted by a tough looking butch bouncer.

"Amelie. *Il me fait plaisir de te revoir.*"

"*Bonsoir.* It's good to see you, too. This is Jesse. From America."

"Hello, Jesse."

She stamped both their hands and they walked in. Jesse felt like she had been transported back to the seventies. There was a large mirrored ball hanging from the ceiling with several smaller ones around the bar. She and Amelie walked to the bar to get drinks.

"What do you drink?" Jesse asked.

"Champagne."

Jesse balked, but figured what the hell? She was on a date with a hot woman and if that's what the lady wanted, that's what she'd get.

"What kind?"

"I'll order. You pay. What will you drink?"

"A Kronenbourg."

Amelie spoke to the bartender in French and turned to hand Jesse her beer. She moved out of the way so Jesse could pay.

They walked to a table and sat to sip their drinks.

"Will you not ask me to dance?" Amelie finally said.

"I'd love to dance with you."

"Come, then."

Jesse allowed Amelie to lead her onto the floor where they danced to one song after another. The music seemed to be a part of Amelie as she turned and twisted in rhythm. Jesse could hold her own on the floor, but often found herself simply watching Amelie.

The music slowed and Amelie moved into Jesse's arms.

"This is nice, no?"

"This is very nice."

Amelie's head rested on Jesse's shoulder as their bodies molded together. Jesse rested her head on Amelie's and forced herself to keep her hands on her waist, though she wanted, with every ounce of her, to place them on her shapely backside.

The song ended and Amelie didn't move out of Jesse's arms. Instead she looked into her eyes and pulled her closer. Jesse lowered her mouth until their lips met. The kiss was soft, tender, and brief, but it sent shock waves coursing through her body. She pulled up as Amelie stepped away. She was craving more, but wasn't going to push Amelie. She could only hope.

They went back to their table.

"You kiss nice," Amelie said.

"So do you," Jesse said. "So tell me. Where did you learn to speak English?"

"In school. So many Americans come here. English is necessary. You really speak no French?"

"None. But I have a feeling I'll be learning some."

"You should. Much easier to get around then."

"Yes."

They danced a few more fast songs and then another slow. After the slow song, it was Jesse who held tight. She bent to taste Amelie's lips again. This time Amelie opened her mouth and welcomed Jesse in. Jesse tentatively moved her tongue inside, tasting the sweet champagne.

She pulled Amelie closer and pressed them together. The feel of Amelie's body against hers made her legs buckle. She moved her hands over Amelie's back and down to cup her ass. It was soft and firm at the same time. Jesse wanted more.

"Let's get out of here," Jesse said.

"Where to?"

"My place," Jesse said.

"It is small, no?"

"All we need is a bed."

"You are bad."

"Am I?"

"I'm sure you are good, too."

"I'm sure you are, too."

Jesse hailed a cab and the two were in each other's arms before it even pulled away from the curb. They kissed passionately, mouths open, tongues entwined. Jesse fought to keep her hands on top of Amelie's clothes, though the need to touch her was overwhelming.

When they reached her apartment, Jesse fumbled with her passcard. She was shaking with her need for Amelie. She finally got the doors open and took Amelie's hand. They took the stairs two at a time and were both breathless when they reached Jesse's room.

Jesse let them in and took Amelie's blouse over her head. She stripped her bra next and bent to kiss her supple breasts. Amelie dug her nails into Jesse's back, urging her on. She sucked on one nipple and then the other, hungry for more.

Amelie pulled away.

"We must get naked," she said. "I want to see you."

Jesse was in a fog of desire, but the words cut through it. She stood back and quickly undressed, then helped Amelie out of the rest of her clothes. She took a moment to admire the beauty of her body before leading her to the bedroom.

They fell onto the bed, kissing and stroking each other. Jesse tried to take the lead and rub between Amelie's legs, but Amelie was just as intent to get at her. She finally gave up and lay on her back, allowing Amelie to have her way first.

"You are so handsome," Amelie said. "Your body was made to love."

"As was yours. Please, let me at you."

"You must wait. Patience, *mon ami*."

Patience was the last thing Jesse wanted at the moment, but she tried. She closed her eyes and allowed herself to simply feel. Amelie was a talented lover and soon replaced her hand with her mouth between Jesse's legs.

"Oh dear God, that feels good," Jesse said. She moved her hips in time with Amelie's tongue, rubbing it all over herself. "Oh yes. Don't stop. Oh God, Amelie. Please don't stop."

She felt the knot tighten in her stomach as every molecule of energy came together deep inside. She clenched her fists as her body convulsed when the climax crashed over her.

"That was nice, no?" Amelie asked when she climbed up next to Jesse.

"That was wonderful," Jesse said. "Absolutely amazing. And now it's your turn."

Jesse kissed Amelie hard on the mouth, tasting her own orgasm there. She moved her hand to cup a small but firm breast. Her fingers quickly closed on a nipple, which she tugged and twisted.

A small moan escaped Amelie and Jesse smiled. She kissed Amelie's neck and shoulder while she moved her hand lower. She found Amelie wet and ready for her.

"You feel so wonderful," Jesse murmured. "You're so hot and wet."

"Yes. Take me, Jesse."

Jesse did as she was asked and in a matter of minutes, Amelie cried out as she came.

"You are a talented lover, Jesse."

"As are you."

"We are good together."

Jesse felt the cold grip her stomach. Surely Amelie didn't think they had a future.

"You are quiet, Jesse. What is on your mind?"

"Well, I just, I mean, I don't know what to think."

"To think? What about?"

"You said we're good together," Jesse said.

"We are. Good sex is always fun."

"But that's all it was?"

"Oh Jesse. I don't want to hurt you. But I don't want anything permanent. I want fun."

"Oh, okay. I wasn't sure."

"I'm sorry. I should go."

Jesse didn't know what to say. Clearly, Amelie thought she was the one who wanted more and she didn't, but was there a point to making that clear?

"I'll walk you out and call you a cab," Jesse said. "I'll see you at the market, huh?"

"Yes, you will. Thank you for tonight. It was fun."

With Amelie safely in the cab and heading for home, Jesse let herself back in her apartment and fell into a satisfied sleep.

Jesse woke late the next morning. The memories of the previous evening had already started to fade. She tried to find her excitement and desire to explore, but she felt empty. She missed Sara terribly. It would have been so fun to share this magical city with the love of her life.

She rolled over and pulled the covers over her head, but sleep wouldn't come back to her. She finally gave up and got out of bed. She padded to the kitchen, but couldn't find her motivation to even make coffee. She pulled some clothes on and walked across the street to the café.

Jesse sat at the table waiting for the waitress. She was surprised when Odette walked over.

"What's wrong, my friend Jesse? You look sad."

"I'm sorry. I'm not very good company today."

Odette walked off and Jesse sat alone in her misery. Odette was right back with a pot of coffee and two cups. She sat across from Jesse and filled their cups.

"Talk to me. Odette's a good listener."

"I really am sorry, but I don't feel like talking."

She sipped her coffee. It was bitter, but felt good. She knew she shouldn't be rude to Odette. She decided to try.

"Have you ever been in love, Odette?"

"Oh, Jesse. Paris is the city of love."

"So, I've heard. But have you ever been truly in love?"

"Yes, Jesse. Once upon a time. It was wonderful."

Jesse just nodded.

"And you? You have, I take it?" Odette asked.

"Yes. And she was amazing."

"And you grew apart? Or what?"

Jesse took another sip of coffee. She tried to steady her voice.

"She died."

"Oh, Jesse. I'm so sorry. When?"

"Four years ago. I miss her."

"I am sure you do. Why today so much?"

"I don't know. I've enjoyed the few days I've had here. But I just woke up this morning wishing she was here with me enjoying this beautiful city."

"You will be better when you get in school. It will keep your mind busy, no?"

"I hope so."

"I will bring you a big breakfast. You'll feel better," Odette said.

"I'm not really that hungry, Odette."

"Food cures all, Jesse. You relax. Odette will be back."

Jesse watched her walk off and mentally berated herself for making such an ass of herself. She was sure Odette thought she was pathetic. She should have just stayed home instead of venturing out in the mood she was in.

Odette was back in a few minutes with bacon and eggs. Once again, she sat across from Jesse and picked up her coffee.

The smell of the food was too much and Jesse dug in. It was like heaven on her taste buds.

"This is delicious."

"I told you. Odette always knows what's best."

Jesse just nodded, her mouth full of food.

"So tell me, Jesse. What have you seen so far?"

"I've been to the Champs Elysees twice now. Once during the day at the shopping district. And then last night to a restaurant and a club."

"Ah. Are you maybe a little hung over this morning?"

"No." Jesse laughed. "I'm fine that way."

"There. That's better. You have a great laugh."

Jesse leaned back against the booth.

"You sure are easy to talk to, Odette."

"We're going to be good friends, Jesse. I knew this the first time I saw you."

"I'd like that, Odette."

"Tonight we'll go out, yes?"

"We will?" Jesse's heart raced. The idea really appealed to her.

"We'll go to a park to listen to some music. You like music?"

"I do."

"Then be here at eight and we'll go."

"Where?"

"There is a park close enough to walk. They play music Friday nights. Tonight is what you Americans call Jazz. You like jazz?"

"I love jazz."

"We will listen then. And dance if we want."

"Thanks, Odette. That sounds like just what I need."

"I must get to work. I will see you tonight."

Jesse finished and paid, then walked back to her apartment. She was feeling mixed emotions. The idea of spending time with Odette had her really excited, which made her feel guilty. She was confused. She never felt guilty when she was with a woman, so why with Odette? She lay on her bed and stared at the ceiling, thinking of Sara. She missed her so much, but was it time for her to move on? And who said anything about getting serious with Odette?

She fell asleep and woke a few hours later, groggy and more confused. She showered to wake up. After, she contemplated calling it off with Odette, but she didn't want to. She was looking forward to that night more than any date she had had in a very long time.

At promptly eight o'clock, she walked into the café to find Odette seated at a table drinking coffee.

"You are an American," Odette laughed.

"How so?"

"I said eight and here you are at eight. Most Parisians would wander in later."

"I learned that last night. I can't help it, though. I'm usually early."

"That is fine. It suits you. You look very nice. That blue shirt accents your eyes."

Jesse was flattered and found herself tongue-tied at the compliment. She took in Odette's tan Capri's and green boat neck shirt.

"You look very stunning yourself."

"My new friend is a charmer, no?"

"No. I just tell it like it is."

"Let us go hear the music, my friend," Odette said. She picked up a blanket that was next to her on the seat and stood.

"Yes, let's."

They left the café and Odette casually looped her arm through Jesse's. The feel of her so close caused Jesse's hormones to race. She cautioned herself to keep calm. She had no way of knowing how the night would end and she didn't need to get worked up for nothing. She told herself to just relax and enjoy Odette's company.

They walked five blocks and came to a small park the size of a city block. It was bordered in trees with several more growing in the park. The lawn was verdant and inviting. The music was excellent and Jesse soon felt the worries of the day washing away.

Odette spread the blanket and they sat to watch the people and listen to the music.

"Next time we will be more prepared," Odette said.

"What do you mean?"

"We will bring wine and cheese and baguettes."

"Oh, what a great idea."

"Next Friday we will do that," Odette said.

"It's a date." As soon as she said it, Jesse felt foolish. Maybe Odette didn't consider this a date.

"Yes, it is. Are you enjoying yourself so far?"

"I am." Jesse breathed a sigh of relief. "So, Odette, you told me last night you never take breaks. What is this?"

"This is different."

Jesse waited for her to expand on the statement, but she didn't. That's all she said, leaving Jesse to wonder what was different. She jumped to her own conclusions. She decided that Odette was into her. And that worked for her.

Jesse studied Odette watching the people around her. She sat with her legs stretched out in front of her, crossed at the ankles. Her feet moved in time to the music and her head never stopped looking from one group of people to another.

"You enjoy people watching?" Jesse asked.

"Oh, very much. And you?"

"Oh yeah. I think every artist does. It's where we get so much of our inspiration."

"I think maybe I was an artist in a former life," Odette said.

"Maybe you were."

"I sure like them now."

Jesse swallowed hard and searched for something intelligent to say.

"So tell me, when the school is in session, is the café so crowded it'll be hard to get a seat?"

"It gets busy during the usual, um, rush times. You know, lunch and dinner."

"And breakfast?"

"I find that you artists do not like to get up early." She laughed.

"Not even when we have classes?"

"I foresee you sleeping until the last minute. Then going to class."

"I foresee me stopping in for coffee before class."

"We'll see who's right, won't we?" Odette said.

"Would you like to dance?" Jesse finally worked up the nerve to ask.

"I'd love to."

They cut through the crowd to the section of the park designated for dancing. It was a small section of concrete among the vibrant greens and browns. Odette moved into Jesse's arms and at that moment, all was right in the world. Jesse seldom danced ballroom style, as she called it, but she held Odette with one hand around her waist and her other hand up with Odette's in it. They moved easily together, swaying to the gentle beats the band put out.

"You are a good dancer. Someone has much experience," Odette said.

"You're easy to dance with."

They danced to several songs, then walked back to the blanket hand in hand.

"So, tell me, Jesse. Where are you from in America?"

"Houston."

"That is a small city, no?"

Jesse laughed.

"It's the fourth largest city in the States."

"No!"

"Yes. It truly is."

"I have not met many people from Houston. Are there a lot of artists there?"

"I don't know. I wasn't really active in the community."

"No? I thought all artists lived in communes with other artists in the States." Odette laughed.

"You're just messing with me now," Jesse said.

Odette kept laughing. The sound was music to Jesse's ears.

"Have you ever been to the States?"

"Sadly, I have not," Odette said. "I long to go. Someday I will."

"I hope you get there."

"So, Jesse, tell me about your life in Houston outside of the commune. And how did you end up in Paris?"

"There's not a lot to tell. I had your basic nine-to-five job. I dabbled in art. One day a friend convinced me to show some art at a local show. Very low key. It was in a city park. And an art dealer came by and liked my work. And I ended up here. That's about it."

"How exciting. So you were not serious about your art?"

"No. It was just a hobby."

"What art dealer found you?"

"Her name is Constance Moriarty."

"Ah, yes. Constance Moriarty. She is a patron of the arts. She is a, um, classy lady." Odette smiled.

"Yes, she is."

"She is good to have on your side," Odette said.

"How well do you know her?" Jesse was curious and somewhat jealous, knowing how Constance liked attractive women.

"I have met her at school functions. I go to them occasionally to support students who are patrons of the café."

Jesse decided they didn't have a history and relaxed somewhat. Though she still didn't understand why she would be jealous of either woman.

"Tell me about yourself, Odette. How did you come to own your café? Are you originally from Paris?"

"I am from a small village in northern France. I came to Paris as a young woman and fell in love with the city. I worked in restaurants until I could afford my own café."

"You must be very proud of your place."

"I am. It is my life and my love, as I said. Let's dance some more now, Jesse."

They danced several more songs and Jesse never wanted the night to end. She still had no inkling from Odette just how it might end. She wanted to take her home, but would be just as happy to know they would go out again next Friday night.

The dances ended and Odette placed her hand on Jesse's arm.

"My dear Jesse, I'm having so much fun, but I must tell you, it's getting late. I need to get up early in the morning. Will you walk me back to the café now?"

"Sure, Odette."

They strolled back to the café and Jesse was sad to say good night to Odette.

"I'll see you at the café, yes?" Odette said.

"Definitely. And next Friday we'll go back to the park?"

"Yes, Jesse. I'd like that." She kissed Jesse's cheek and let herself in the café.

Jesse walked back to her apartment, missing Odette already.

CHAPTER ELEVEN

Jesse woke the next morning feeling melancholy. She really enjoyed her night with Odette and wanted to spend more time with her. But how could she tell if Odette felt the same way? She seemed to have fun. And she mentioned wanting to see her again. But was she just being nice to the new kid on the block?

She got up and pulled on some clothes. It was a rainy day, but she still wanted to explore the city. She opted to ride the Metro around town to just check out different sections. She spent the day exploring the major spots in the city and was falling more in love with the city at every stop.

As the afternoon wore on, the pull to see the Louvre was strong. She hopped on the line that would take her there and stood in awe in front of the museum. She couldn't believe she was in front of one of the premier art museums of the world. The pyramid was magnificent, even in the rain. She couldn't wait to get inside.

The place was crowded, but not as bad as she'd expected. She paid her entry fees and walked into the large, vaulted ceilinged building. She scanned her map and found where the baroque paintings were. Her stomach had butterflies as she made her way to view the work of the masters.

She viewed the paintings, carefully scanning them to observe the brushstrokes and lighting techniques used in their creation. She was in heaven and dared to dream, even briefly, that someday her art would hang on the walls of a museum.

Jesse found her way to the renaissance section next and scoured the paintings there, as well. She lost herself in the beauty that surrounded her. She finally came to the *Mona Lisa* and stood glued to her spot. There it was. The consummate work of art was just feet from her. She couldn't get close to it, but that didn't matter. She was looking at it. She felt the goose flesh cover her at the magnitude of the moment. She knew she was where she needed to be. She had made the right choice. Art was more than a hobby for her. It was a passion. And she deserved to pursue it.

She spent the rest of the afternoon and into the evening at the museum, seeing all the famous works. She was both exhausted and exhilarated as she caught the Metro back to her apartment. Her apartment felt small and empty after all she'd seen that day and she didn't want to be alone. She showered and dressed and walked across the street.

The café was crowded and she took the last open table. She saw Odette talking to people several tables over. She knew she hadn't seen her, but she wished she would come over and talk to her. Maybe eventually she would.

Giselle arrived at her table with a beer.

"I'm that predictable, huh?" Jesse said.

"You need a beer with dinner. I know this."

"Well, thank you."

"Do you know what you'd like for dinner?"

"I don't yet. I'm sorry."

"No problem. We are busy, but I'll be back as soon as I can."

Giselle disappeared and Jesse sat in her booth nursing her beer. She wished she had a pen so she could doodle on a napkin. She was sure she would make art of some kind that night.

"You are back? You don't cook for yourself?" Jesse looked up at the soft voice to see Odette's kind, questioning gaze.

"Oh, Odette. I had such an amazing day. I feel so alive. I didn't want to be alone in my apartment, so I came over here for dinner."

"I want to hear about your day, but we are so busy right now. Can you come back tonight and talk to me?"

"Sure." Jesse hoped she didn't sound as overzealous as she felt. "When?"

"Can you come back at ten?"

"I'd love to."

"Good. We will chat then."

Jesse ate dinner and went back home to kill the time. She ached to paint, but the lighting in her apartment left much to be desired. Still, she got out her easel and paints and began a painting of the stores on the Champs Elysees and the shoppers she'd seen. She blurred the paints well to show crowds and was happy with how well she captured the buildings.

It was finally almost ten, so she put everything away and walked back to the café, still high on her energy from the day.

"Oh, good." Odette greeted her with a kiss on the cheek. "You came back."

"I said I would."

"One never knows, though."

Jesse thought the statement odd. Why wouldn't she have come back to see Odette? She wouldn't miss any time with her. Should she let her know that? Surely it was obvious, or so she thought.

"I wasn't about to miss this time with you."

"Dear Jesse. You are a sweet woman."

"I'm an honest woman, Odette."

Odette poured them each a cup of coffee, adding some cream liqueur to them.

"So, tell me about your wonderful day."

"I went to the Louvre today."

"How exciting. Tell me what you saw, how you felt. I want to know everything."

"I saw everything. I saw sculptures and paintings. Oh, Odette, the paintings." She shook her head, marveling anew at all she'd seen.

"What is it like to see them through an artist's eyes?"

"It was amazing. The work those artists put into their creations was phenomenal. To see the brushstrokes still admired centuries later...what a rush."

"You are like a little child. Your eyes are bright with excitement. Your cheeks flushed. It is a good look on you."

Jesse felt herself blush at the words. She was sure she sounded like a little kid after her first trip to Disneyland. But she didn't care. She was so happy, she almost missed the compliment at the end of Odette's words.

"Thank you. I feel so alive. It's been a long time since I've felt this good."

"I'm so happy for you, Jesse."

"Thank you."

"We should celebrate," Odette said.

"I thought we were." Jesse held up her liqueur laced coffee.

"Oh, no. That's just to take the edge off the caffeine. You wait here. I'll be right back."

Odette returned with a chilled bottle of champagne and two flutes.

"I keep this for special occasions. And this is definitely one."

She handed the bottle to Jesse, who skillfully opened it and poured two glasses.

Odette held up her glass.

"To new beginnings."

"Indeed." Jesse tapped Odette's glass with her own and took a sip. It was smooth and cool, which helped ease the heat she felt coursing through her. She longed to pull Odette to her and kiss her. Something about this woman really pulled her.

"What are you thinking?" Odette asked.

"Huh? Why?"

"Your eyes got dark. Very dark. And your look was very seductive, if I may say so."

"I'm sorry. Just thinking how nice this is."

"It's very nice. You're an easy person to be with, Jesse."

"As are you."

"Thank you."

They sipped their champagne in silence, which Jesse didn't find comfortable at all. She felt like she should say something, but couldn't think of what.

"So tell me, Jesse," Odette broke the silence. "What was your favorite part of the Louvre?"

"The *Mona Lisa*," Jesse answered easily. "Such a piece of history and so beautiful."

"It is a shame you can't see it up close, is it not?"

"Still, it was such an honor to be able to see it at all. But all the paintings were amazing. They gave me hope and allowed me to dream."

"Everyone should dream, Jesse."

Odette poured more champagne for them.

"Are you looking forward to school on Monday?"

"I am. I don't know what to expect, but I'm excited. I can't wait to hone my skills."

"Someday I'll say I knew you when."

Jesse looked at Odette, who smiled at her. She didn't know what to say.

"You will be a rich and famous artist in the States. But you'll come back and visit Odette, yes?"

"Of course."

"Good. Now come. Sit next to me."

Jesse didn't know if she trusted herself that close to Odette, but she didn't want to be rude. She sat down and Odette sidled up against her. They poured the last of the champagne into their glasses.

"What shall we toast to now?" Odette asked.

"Special friends," Jesse said.

"I like that. To special friends."

They sipped their champagne and Odette put her glass down. She turned to face Jesse, who was feeling a fog of champagne and desire.

"I should go," Jesse said.

"No, my Jesse. You should relax."

"I don't know," Jesse said.

"I am a big girl," Odette said. "I trust you and I trust me. You need to trust me, too."

"I don't know if I trust me," Jesse said.

Odette stroked Jesse's cheek. Jesse closed her eyes and tried to think clearly.

"Do you want to kiss me, Jesse?"

Jesse opened her eyes and saw the desire in Odette's. She nodded.

"Then, please. Kiss me."

Jesse cupped Odette's jaw and ran her thumb over her soft cheek. Something was happening and she wasn't sure what. She knew she had to kiss Odette. God knew she wanted to, but there was something else she was feeling and she couldn't put her finger on it.

She leaned into Odette slowly, needing to drag out the moment. Her heart was pounding in her chest as she watched Odette slowly close her eyes. She closed her own just before their lips met. The kiss was soft and sensual. She felt Odette's arms circle her neck and pull her close. The kiss intensified and soon it was all Jesse could do not to lean Odette back in the booth and climb on top of her.

The kiss finally ended and they rested forehead to forehead, each trying to catch her breath.

"That was some kiss, Jesse."

"Yes. Yes, it was. Thank you for that."

"How long will I have to wait for another one?"

Jesse kissed her again, full of confidence and passion. When that kiss ended, Odette smiled at her.

"I wasn't expecting that, but it was nice."

"So, can I see you again?" Jesse asked.

"We have another date Friday, no?"

"Yes. Yes, we do. I suppose I can wait that long."

Odette laughed.

"Oh, my Jesse. You will be so busy with school this week. And I won't be a distraction for you."

"Yes, you will," Jesse said.

"Thank you for that," Odette smiled. "But I mean I won't allow myself to distract you from your studies. You will come in to the café when you can and we will see each other, but we will behave. And Friday we will have another date."

"So if I come here every day you won't think I'm a creeper?"

"A what?"

"A stalker. A weirdo."

Odette laughed.

"Oh, no. I will always be happy to see you. But if you cannot come in, that is okay, too. I will know you are busy."

"You're something special, Odette."

She watched the blush creep up Odette's face.

"So are you, Jesse."

They finished their champagne and Jesse rose to leave.

"Thank you for tonight," she said. "For all of it."

"Thank you. And I truly am glad you had such a wonderful day."

They hugged at the door and Jesse walked home. Her mind was filled with Odette and her wonderful kisses as she stripped for bed. She wished Odette was with her, but at the same time was happy she wasn't. There was something different about her, and Jesse was content to relax and see where things went.

Jesse woke early the next morning and fought the urge to head across the street to see Odette. Instead, she made herself coffee and bacon and eggs. She got out her sketchpad and drew some of the buildings she'd seen. Downtown Paris spoke to her like no other city had. She was in love with the Renaissance architecture and wanted to capture it perfectly. She worked and worked until her stomach started growling.

It was two o'clock and she couldn't believe it was already that late. But she was hungry and reasoned it was a decent time to go across the street. Odette would be happy to see her, right? Part of her wondered if there was a new favorite student for Odette every year. But she didn't seem the type. Jesse convinced herself Odette really liked her as she showered and dressed.

She had on khaki cargo pants and a black golf shirt. She was casual, but knew she looked nice. Black was a good color on her. Or so she'd been told.

She walked into an almost empty café. She quickly glanced around, but didn't see Odette. Her heart sank. Still, she needed food and that's what she was there for.

A new waitress came over, and she ordered a beer and the special. She didn't know what the special was, but figured it couldn't be bad. So far, everything she'd tried had been delicious.

"How did I not see you come in?" Jesse heard the soft voice as she felt the light touch on her shoulder. She turned to look into the smiling gaze of Odette.

"I don't know. I didn't see you when I came in either."

"I must have been in the office. My work is never done."

"You must be tired today. You were up late last night."

"Tired? Perhaps a little. But happy."

"Good."

"And what have you done with your day so far?"

"I've been sketching."

"Oh, good. I hope I get to see some of your work some time."

"I'm sure you will."

"I will leave you to your lunch. Enjoy." She squeezed Jesse's shoulder and walked off.

Jesse sat there, happy as can be to have spoken to Odette even briefly. She wondered what was wrong with her, but didn't care. She knew what her next sketch would be of. She paid her bill and hurried home.

She opened her sketchpad to a clean page and grabbed her pencils. First, she sketched the outline. It was neither a perfect circle, nor a perfect oval. Rather, it was somewhere in between. Whatever it was, the shape was perfect. Next, she added the perfectly shaped ears before shading the cheekbones. Then it was time to sketch the captivating green eyes. The hair was last, and when the sketch was complete, it was the spitting image of Odette.

Jesse smiled her approval and checked her watch. It was close to midnight. She couldn't believe how long it had taken. But it was perfect. She wondered if she should give it to Odette as a present, but thought she might want to keep it for herself. She propped it up on her desk and went to bed.

Sunday morning, Jesse was a bundle of nerves. School would start the next day, and she was no more ready than she had been the first night she met with Constance. She reviewed her class list and finally decided to look around the campus to acclimate herself to a degree.

Her first order of business was the bookstore, which she found just south of the commons. She bought the supplies she would need for her classes, though she'd brought most of her own with her. Still, these were required, so she bought them with the credit card Constance had given her. She took her purchases and wandered the grounds, trying to find which buildings her classes were in. Satisfied she had a handle on things, she went home and put her supplies in the closet.

Knowing she would be too busy to shop the next week, she decided to head to the open-air market and pick up a few items. She was surprised at how busy it was and realized it was more than just a market. There were many more stalls that day with artisans offering their wares. There were potters and candlemakers, jewelers and painters. She could feel the pulse of life coursing through the stalls.

She bought some bread and cheese and was walking toward the wine section when she heard someone call her.

"Jesse the American!"

She turned to see Amelie at her flower cart.

"Do you ever take days off?" Jesse asked her.

"Why would I? A girl needs to make money."

"Well, good luck!"

"Will you not buy flowers today?"

"I will be back on Friday and buy flowers then," Jesse said.

"Do you have a date? I told you, Paris is the city of love."

Jesse laughed.

"I do have a date and I will get flowers. I'll see you then."

She picked up some wine to keep in her apartment and bought some more eggs then headed back home. She put everything away and the now familiar restlessness set in. She tried to tell herself to stay away, but she couldn't. She went across the street for dinner.

"Surely you know how to cook," Giselle joked with her.

"I do, but it's so easy to come over here."

"Do you even have food in your home?"

"I do," Jesse said again. "I even went shopping today."

"You have a crush on ol' Giselle, don't you?"

Jesse started laughing as Giselle turned to leave.

"What's so funny?" Odette walked over just then.

"Giselle says I must have a crush on her since I'm over here all the time."

"Maybe you do have a crush on someone," Odette said.

"Maybe I do." Jesse felt brave.

"I like that." Odette smiled.

"So do I."

"How was your day?"

"It was good. I checked out the Academy and then went to the market. A low-key day."

"Good. Tomorrow is a big day."

"I know," Jesse said. "I'm so excited."

"I need to mingle, Jesse. I will see you sometime next week?"

"I'm sure I'll be in tomorrow for dinner to report in about my first day."

"Why not come by at ten again and we'll talk alone."

"That sounds great. I'll do that."

"I look forward to it." Odette winked at her before walking off, sending Jesse's heart racing like a runaway horse.

CHAPTER TWELVE

Jesse was at her first class by seven forty-five Monday morning. Her eight o'clock class was The Renaissance of the Arts. She was looking forward to studying the history and artists of that period. The class was easy that day, with the teacher simply taking roll and handing out a syllabus. He asked if anyone had any questions and, when no one did, dismissed the class at eight fifteen.

So, with her first class under her belt and nothing to do until ten, Jesse wandered down the street to the café. It wasn't very busy. Apparently, Odette had been right about students sleeping in.

"You are here early." Odette greeted her, kissing her on her cheek.

"My first class got out early. My next class isn't for two hours so I thought I'd grab a cup of coffee."

"Have a seat. I'll bring it myself."

Jesse sat facing the counter, so she could watch Odette. She enjoyed the easy way Odette moved, never seemingly overly hurried no matter how chaotic the place was. And this morning, she was moving even easier. Jesse felt an unfamiliar pull in her stomach. There was no denying her attraction to Odette, but there was more and she just couldn't figure it out.

Odette turned back to her with the coffee and raised an eyebrow at Jesse, who had just been busted for staring.

"You like what you see, *mon ami*?" Odette teased her.

Jesse blushed and took a coffee cup from Odette. Odette sat across from her with a cup of her own.

"You don't mind if I join you?"

"Not at all. I'd enjoy that."

"So why are you not still in your first class again?"

"He let us go early. I guess school will start in earnest tomorrow."

"And what is your next class?"

"Still life drawing. I hope we get to use our new supplies today."

"I hope so, too. Which do you prefer, Jesse? Painting or sketching?"

"It depends on my mood. I love both."

"Must you, um, specialize in one or the other when you are a famous artist?"

"I don't know. I've never really thought about it. If I had to do only one, I suppose I'd paint. But I'll always sketch, if even just for myself."

"Good. You must always do what your heart wants."

Jesse sipped her coffee and pondered that statement. It had been so long since her heart had wanted to do anything but grieve that she didn't even know if she'd be able to listen to it if it sent her messages again.

"You are a deep person, my Jesse."

"Why do you say that?"

"You, um, disappear sometimes. Inside your head. I'd love to know what you think at times like that, but I understand those thoughts are yours and yours alone."

"I'm sorry. I don't mean to be rude."

"You are never rude. Thoughtful is not rude. It is quite all right."

"This coffee is really good," Jesse said in an attempt to change the subject.

"Thank you. The company is quite nice, too."

"Yes, it is," Jesse said. "I'm glad you were able to join me."

"It's a rare treat for me to sit down during the day."

"So you've said. I'm honored you would take a break with me."

"I like you, Jesse. Do I need to tell you this?"

Jesse's heart sped up again. Her palms got damp and she wiped them on her jeans.

"I kind of got that from the other night," she said, then felt like she sounded lame. "I mean, I was kind of hoping you didn't treat all your patrons that way. I mean..."

Odette laughed. It was a soft, gentle laugh that made Jesse's crotch spasm.

"It's okay, Jesse. No. I don't do that with others. Just you."

Jesse braced herself for the familiar desire to run, but it didn't come. Instead, all she wanted to do was pull Odette to her and kiss her again.

"I'm glad. That makes me happy," Jesse said.

"It makes me happy, too."

The café was filling up and Odette excused herself.

"I must get back to work now. It was wonderful seeing you. You'll still come by tonight?"

"Definitely."

"I'll see you then."

Jesse watched Odette walk off and couldn't wipe the smile from her face.

She made her way back to campus and arrived at the classroom for her sketch class. It was a small classroom, with old-fashioned desks that wrapped around the student. Now she felt like she was in school again.

In the front of the class was a table with some fruit on it. The teacher walked in and introduced himself. He told the class to get out their supplies and sketch the fruit.

Jesse went to work and soon had the outlines of the pear, apple, and banana on her page. She sketched the shadows and colored in the rest of the fruit. She looked at her page and then at the plate. She thought she'd done a good job. She glanced up at the clock. It was almost noon.

"Write your names in the upper right hand corner and leave your work on your desk," the teacher said. "You're dismissed."

Jesse did as she was instructed and left the classroom feeling good about her first real class. She should be able to ace this one, anyway.

The next two classes she had were much like the first. Only her sketching class had taken its allotted time. She knew classes would start in earnest the next day, but she was happy for a light first day, since it had been years since she'd been at school.

She got back to her apartment and sent Liza a quick e-mail telling her about her day. She got an e-mail back from her, so they corresponded for a while before Liza got busy at work. With nothing pressing, Jesse lay down and took a nap.

She woke several hours later, feeling refreshed and hungry. She went to her kitchen and made herself a light dinner. It felt good to be cooking for herself. It had been too long. Sara used to do all the cooking for them and while she'd always been able to cook, the desire to do so had been long gone. Still, she knew she had to get used to it. She was on a budget and had to be careful how much money she spent at the café, no matter how strong the pull was to eat every meal there.

After dinner, Jesse took another shower and dressed quickly, excited to see Odette. Their kisses from the other night were still burned into her brain. She was hoping for more of the same. Although, without the champagne, how affectionate would Odette be?

She arrived at the café to find it dark. Her heart sank. Had Odette forgotten? She tried the door and it was unlocked, so she walked in.

"Oh, my Jesse. You are here." Odette was sitting at a table with a candle burning on it.

"I am. I was worried. I thought you had forgotten."

"No, my dear. I just thought I'd set the mood."

"I like the mood," Jesse said.

"Good. Now sit with me. Tell me about your day."

Jesse stood by the booth, not sure which side to slide in on.

"You may sit next to me, if you'd like," Odette said.

Jesse slid in next to her and took her hand. She felt like a high school kid again. It was a nice feeling.

"My day was pretty nondescript," Jesse said.

"I'm sorry. I don't know that word," Odette said.

"It means there wasn't a lot exciting going on. There's not a lot to tell."

"No? Nothing happened?"

"Well, in Still Life Drawing, we sketched some fruit. I'm pretty sure I aced that. The rest of the classes just took attendance and let us go early."

"So, you are disappointed in your first day at the *Academie?*"

"Oh no. Not at all. It was nice to have an easy first day. I'm sure the next few days will be overwhelming."

"But not too overwhelming, I hope?" Odette said.

"Not too much." Jesse laughed. "My brain just has to get used to studying and learning."

"You have a good brain, Jesse. I can tell. You are an intelligent woman."

"Thank you, Odette. I try."

Odette nuzzled Jesse's neck.

"You smell good, Jesse."

Jesse leaned her head back and let the sensations wash over her. When she could take no more, she took Odette's face in her hands.

"May I kiss you again?" she asked.

"I was hoping you would."

Jesse claimed Odette's mouth with her own, softly, tentatively, as if it were the first kiss they'd shared.

"You are so gentle, my Jesse," Odette said. "I love how you kiss."

"Mm. I love kissing you, Odette." She kissed her again, applying pressure to her lips with her tongue. Odette opened her mouth and welcomed her in. They kissed together for what seemed an eternity, until Jesse finally had to come up for air.

"Oh, Jesse. I love how soft and sweet your tongue is in my mouth. I love how you explore me slowly and easily."

Jesse thought she'd overheat at the words. She wanted to explore every inch of Odette that way, but wasn't sure either of them was ready for that.

"So, tell me about your day," Jesse said.

"My day?" Odette laughed. "My day was spent doing what I love and looking forward to tonight."

"I love your honesty," Jesse said, still not sure why the urge to flee hadn't kicked in.

"Didn't you look forward to tonight?" Odette asked.

"I did."

"Good." Odette leaned in and kissed Jesse again, this time with a passion that made Jesse's head spin. She kissed her back and felt the familiar twitching in her crotch. She wanted Odette and wanted her soon.

Odette pulled away.

"We must be careful," Odette said.

Jesse looked around.

"Is someone here to see us?"

"No." Odette laughed. "Nothing like that. We just must be sure we can stop."

"True. We can't get carried away in a booth."

"No. That wouldn't do."

"I wouldn't try that, though. I have too much respect for you."

"Thank you. I know you wouldn't, but when we kiss...*ooo la la*."

"My thoughts exactly," Jesse said.

"And now, my Jesse, we must say good night. We both have big days tomorrow."

"Is something going on for you tomorrow?" Jesse asked.

"Just work. Every day is a big day for me."

"Okay. Well, thank you for inviting me over tonight."

"Thank you for coming."

Odette walked Jesse to the door. They kissed again before Jesse said good night and went home.

She tossed and turned in bed. She tried to tell herself it was because she'd taken a nap earlier, but she knew better. She had Odette on the brain and everywhere else in her body. Every ounce of her wanted to take Odette. She knew Odette wanted it, too. But when would it happen? How long could Jesse wait? She chided herself to just relax and give it time. Things would happen as they were supposed to. She finally fell into a deep sleep filled with green eyes and a charming smile.

The rest of the week passed in a blur for Jesse. She went to class, came home and studied, and visited the café at least daily. Her teacher had critiqued her sketch of the fruits rather harshly, so she strove harder to study lighting and placement. She was determined to get it right. The historical classes were exciting, but the homework was daunting. She was on her laptop until late every night.

Friday evening finally arrived, and the rest of the week was forgotten. All that was on Jesse's mind was her date with Odette. She went to the market and bought a baguette and some cheese for their picnic. Odette had said she'd bring the wine.

Jesse wandered through the market until she found Amelie.

"Amelie," she said. "I would like to buy some flowers for a friend."

"Roses?" Amelie smiled.

"No roses. Just a nice bouquet, please."

Amelie put together a bouquet of purples and blues and handed it to Jesse.

"That's beautiful. Thank you." She paid and turned to leave.

"Good luck," Amelie said.

"Thanks."

Jesse walked the few blocks to the café and walked in to find Odette seated at the front table. She rose when Jesse arrived and took the flowers Jesse offered.

"These are beautiful," Odette said. "We must put them in water right away."

Jesse waited while Odette found a vase and returned. She set them on the table by the cash register and turned to Jesse.

"Shall we?"

"Do you have the wine and blanket?"

"And plastic cups. *Oui*. I'm ready."

They put everything in the bag Jesse had brought and walked toward the park. Jesse could already hear the music.

"What's the variety of music tonight?" she asked.

"Disco."

Jesse laughed.

"Now there's a blast from the past."

"Are you okay with this?"

"I'm fine with it. I love disco."

"Oh, good. I do, too."

The park wasn't as packed as it had been the previous week and they had their pick of spots. They set the blanket down and sat on it. Jesse leaned back so she was lying propped up on her elbow and Odette mirrored her, looking into her eyes.

"Your eyes are so captivating," she said.

"Thank you," Jesse said, trying to come up with something equally romantic to say back.

"You are nervous tonight, *mon ami*?"

"Is it that obvious?"

"What is on your mind? Talk to Odette."

What was on her mind was the burning desire to kiss Odette. She was so close, her lips just inches away. Jesse wanted to taste them again and again. But they were in public. At a park. And even if Paris was the city of love, she doubted if kissing Odette in public would be well received.

"Where did you go? You do that. You get so serious. Share with me, my Jesse."

Jesse rolled onto her back and folded her hands under her head, hoping to ease the tension. But Odette's face was soon over hers, her eyes gazing longingly at her. She lightly traced Jesse's jaw.

"What is wrong? Please. Did I do something?"

"Oh, no. It's nothing like that. It's just…I mean…well…the thing is…I really want to kiss you."

"Okay. And?"

"And I can't very well do that here."

"Why not? Paris is the city of love."

"What will people do or say if they saw us kissing?"

"They would be happy for us. They would say, 'Look at the happy lovers.'"

"But you're a renowned businesswoman. How would that look?"

"You worry too much, my Jesse. You want to kiss me and I want you to kiss me, so you should kiss me. It's really quite simple."

"You want me to kiss you?" Jesse said.

"Of course. I always want you to kiss me. I love your kisses."

Jesse pulled Odette on top of her and kissed her. It was a series of kisses that at once satisfied her need yet left her craving more.

They sat up again with Jesse in a much better mood.

"That really was all that bothered you?" Odette asked. "You have nothing else going on in that busy mind of yours?"

"That was it. I just really wanted to kiss you like crazy."

"I ask only that you not do it at the café. Everywhere else is fair game."

"I like the kisses we've shared at the café." Jesse grinned.

"You know what I mean. During business hours."

"So, you really don't care if someone sees you kissing on me out here?"

"I'm an old out lesbian, Jesse. Most people who know me know that. And if they see me kissing you, probably they'll just be happy for me."

"Good. Now that that's resolved…" Jesse reached into the bag and pulled out the wine bottle and corkscrew. She got the bottle open and poured them each a generous amount. She sipped hers.

"This is really good."

"Not bad for a picnic red, no?"

"No. Not bad at all. Did you want to eat or dance first?" Jesse said.

"Let's sip our wine for a bit. Then we'll dance."

Jesse relaxed as the hits of the yesteryears washed over them. Half the bottle of wine was gone when a Donna Summer song came on and they decided it was time to dance. They danced to one song after another, all of them causing them to laugh at the agelessness of the music.

They finally made their way back to their spot and opened the baguette and cheese. They ate and drank and watched the people around them. Jesse was feeling more at ease as the evening wore on.

They finished their wine and Odette lay back and patted the blanket next to her.

Jesse propped herself up on an elbow again and looked into Odette's eyes.

"May I ask you a question?" Odette said.

"Anything."

"Will you take me home tonight?"

Jesse swallowed hard and stared at Odette. Surely she'd misunderstood.

"You mean walk you back to the café?"

"That is not what I mean."

"Oh, God, Odette. Oh yes, I'd love to." She kissed her hard on the mouth then, all her pent up passion coming through in one kiss. She fought to keep from climbing on top of her and grinding. She wanted Odette with every ounce of her being.

CHAPTER THIRTEEN

They walked hand in hand back up the street, the music forgotten.

"My place is small," Jesse said.

"But it is yours, no?"

"It is mine."

Jesse opened the door to her apartment and showed Odette the kitchen, where she put their picnic supplies. Odette then wandered to the living room while Jesse put things away.

"Oh my God, Jesse. It's beautiful."

Jesse hurried to find Odette looking at the sketch Jesse had done of her. Instantly embarrassed, she shrugged.

"I tried."

"It's perfect. It is like looking in a mirror."

"Thank you."

"May I have it?"

"I was thinking about giving it to you as a present, so sure."

"You do think of me when we're not together. I know this now," Odette said.

"I do, Odette. I think of little else." She opened her arms and Odette stepped into them. She held her gently.

"I like you, Jesse."

"I like you, Odette."

"I am not a one-night stand kind of woman, my Jesse."

"I don't want you to be," Jesse said, realizing the truth of the words as she said them. She wanted something with Odette. And she wanted tonight to be the first of many they would spend together.

Odette lifted her face and Jesse captured her lips in a tender kiss.

"You make my heart soar with your kisses," Odette said.

Jesse kissed her again, pulling her close. She wanted to take Odette into the bedroom and ravish her, but at the same time, wanted to take things slowly. She wanted to make it right.

"Would you like a glass of wine?" Jesse asked.

"That would be nice."

"Make yourself comfortable. I'll be right back."

Jesse poured them each a glass and walked back into the living room to find Odette seated on the couch. She handed one glass to her and sat next to her.

"Why are you so special, my Jesse?" Odette said.

"What do you mean?"

"Why do you touch me as you do?"

"I could ask the same of you."

"Students come and go in my café. I make friends, but none pull me like you."

"And I meet people every day. I have for years. I've never cared for more than a night with anyone in so long."

"I hope you will not forget me after tonight."

"Not a chance, Odette. I'm crazy about you."

"I'm glad."

They kissed again, slowly, as if they had all the time in the world. When the kiss ended, Jesse took Odette's glass and set both glasses on the table. She placed her hands on Odette's face and kissed her again, this time with more need.

Odette snaked her arms around Jesse's neck as the kiss gained fuel. Jesse was lost in the kiss, in the feelings Odette elicited from her. She wanted more. She needed more.

Jesse ran her hands over Odette's back, up and down, forcing herself not to bring them around to the front as she longed to do. The feel of Odette's back was enough to drive her crazy. Who knew what the feel of her breasts would do to her?

Odette ran her hands inside Jesse's collar, lightly playing with the bare skin she found there. Jesse moaned into Odette's mouth. She never realized how sensitive her neck was. But Odette was playing her perfectly. She brought her hands back to cup Odette's face as she continued to kiss her.

"You are such a good kisser," Odette said, finally breaking the kiss.

"So are you. I could kiss you all night long."

"I may hold you to that."

They kissed some more, and it was Odette who pulled away again.

"I need to feel your skin, my Jesse." She tugged on the base of Jesse's shirt, trying to lift it over her head.

Jesse helped her and they got it off, along with her undershirt. She sat bare from the waist up, looking at Odette.

"Now it's your turn," she said. She helped Odette out of her blouse and marveled at the view in front of her. The tops of Odette's breasts teased her over the top of her bra. She ran her fingers over them, making Odette groan with pleasure.

"Should we take this off?" Odette asked.

"Not yet."

Jesse kissed her anew, this time allowing her hands to roam the front of her. She teased Odette's nipples through the bra and cupped her breasts. Soon, she could take no more.

"Now let's get that off," she said.

Jesse held Odette close as they kissed, loving the feel of their skin pressed against each other. She pulled back and lowered her head to lick all over one of Odette's soft breasts. She finally brought her tongue to the nipple and licked it softly.

"You are making me wild," Odette said.

Jesse brought her hand up to caress Odette's other breast while she finally closed her mouth on her nipple. She sucked it lightly, still running her tongue over its tip.

"Oh, Jesse. What you make me feel."

Jesse sat up and looked her in the eye.

"I want to make you feel so many things."

"You do. You will."

They resumed kissing, their hands roaming over each other's body.

"Your body is so lean," Odette said. "I love it."

"And yours is so wonderful," Jesse said. She liked that Odette's body wasn't the picture of perfection. It was the body of a slightly older woman, and Jesse found it stunning.

"Take me to bed, Jesse. I must go to bed with you."

Jesse pulled Odette off the couch and led her to her small bedroom. She wasn't aware of her surroundings, only of the beautiful Odette in front of her.

Odette closed the distance between them. She kissed Jesse passionately as her hands fumbled with the button on Jesse's slacks. She finally got them unbuttoned and unzipped and she peeled them off Jesse. She knelt and slipped her shoes and socks off to pull her pants all the way off. She rested a cheek on her thigh.

"Oh, my Jesse. You are marvelous. Just look at you."

Jesse felt somewhat self-conscious standing there nude in front of Odette. She helped Odette up and kissed her as she managed to get Odette's skirt off. When they stood naked together, Jesse looked at Odette and her breath caught.

"You are so beautiful," she said. "I want to take my time and love you the right way. Everything about you speaks to me, calls to me."

She ran her hand over Odette's face.

"You're so beautiful," she said again.

She kissed Odette once more. It was another slow, unhurried meeting of their tongues. Jesse couldn't believe everything she was feeling. She wanted to please Odette, to be sure, but she wanted so much more. She wanted it to be special, something Odette would always remember.

Odette sat on the bed and took Jesse's hand, pulling her down to sit next to her.

"Jesse. Oh, my Jesse," Odette said. "Tonight will be magical."

"It will be, Odette."

Jesse eased Odette back and rolled on top of her. She brought her leg between Odette's and pressed into her. She kissed her passionately as she felt the wet heat from her center. Odette wrapped her legs and arms around Jesse, fueling her passion.

Jesse explored every inch of Odette, using her fingers and her mouth. There was no spot left undiscovered or unloved. She memorized every peak and valley, every curve and crevice. And through it all, she wanted more, craved more, needed more.

"Oh, my Jesse. My dear, sweet Jesse," Odette finally said. "I don't think I can take any more."

Jesse realized she, too, was exhausted, yet exhilarated.

"I can't get enough of you," she said.

"You've gotten so much of me already," Odette said. "You have worn me out."

"Come here." Jesse pulled Odette into her arms. She held her tight as they drifted into a sound slumber.

The sunlight had only begun to peek through the window when Jesse woke to feel Odette lazily running her hand over her body.

"You are magnificent, my Jesse. Truly magnificent. What an exquisite body you have."

"I feel the same about yours," Jesse said.

"I want to love you, Jesse."

"Please do."

It was Odette's turn to worship and please Jesse, which she did skillfully. Jesse felt like she was made of Jell–O when Odette finished with her.

It was only when Odette was curled in her arms again, that Jesse realized how late it must be.

"Don't you have to work today?" she asked.

Odette laughed mischievously.

"I took the day off," she admitted. "I had hoped last night would end like it did."

"I'm glad it did," Jesse said.

"So am I."

They fell asleep again and when they woke up again, they were both famished.

"I suppose going across the street for breakfast is out of the question," Jesse joked.

"It might be awkward."

"I have bacon and eggs here if you'd like."

"That would be wonderful. Can I help?"

"No way. You relax. It will be an honor cooking for you, my lady."

They ate their breakfast in bed and after, made love for several more hours. They were insatiable. Jesse felt alive again. She didn't want to think about when Odette would have to leave. She was living in the moment, loving every second with Odette.

"Oh, my Jesse," Odette said. "I could get used to this."

"So could I." Jesse nuzzled her neck.

"Do we ever have to get out of this bed again?"

Jesse laughed.

"I suppose at some point we'll get hungry again."

"I am only hungry for your body. And for what you do to mine."

Jesse rolled over and ran her hand between Odette's legs.

"I love this body."

"Oh, Jesse."

Jesse dipped her fingers inside Odette, who gasped.

"Are you okay?" Jesse asked.

"I'm just a little tender. But please, do not stop."

Jesse used a softer touch and gently entered Odette. She found her still wet, which amazed her. She loved that Odette hadn't yet tired of her. She was sure she'd never tire of Odette.

"You tell me if it's too much, okay?" Jesse said.

"I will. Do not worry. I don't think I could get too much from you."

Jesse continued to probe her, coaxing her to a frenzy. When she felt Odette tighten around her, she buried her face in her neck, keeping from crying out herself as she came at Odette's pleasure.

After another short nap, Jesse woke to find Odette watching her.

"What?" she said.

"Just looking at you. You are so peaceful when you sleep."

"Okay." Jesse blushed. "If you say so."

"I do. What shall we do now? I am thinking a shower would be good for us."

"I'd love to shower with you, but unfortunately, my shower is tiny."

"That's okay. I can stand to be away from you for a few minutes." She smiled.

Jesse's heart swelled. She was enjoying Odette more than she thought possible.

"You go first," she said. "There are some towels in the cupboard."

She watched as Odette walked out of the room, already hungry to have her again. When Odette got out of the shower, Jesse got in and took the quickest shower of her life. She didn't like being away from Odette, either.

"What shall we do now?" Jesse asked when they were both dressed.

"I say we go get dinner. There is a restaurant within walking distance. It will be my treat."

"Your treat? I don't know about that."

"Please, Jesse. I want to treat you to a nice restaurant I know of. Someday you will treat me to a favorite of yours. Fair?"

"Fair."

They walked to the restaurant hand in hand. Jesse never wanted to let go of Odette. She wanted to be in constant contact with her. When they reached the restaurant and were sitting across the table from each other, the distance was too great.

"I think you should move over here to sit next to me."

"You do?" Odette said.

"I do."

"I will do that, then. I would like to be closer to you."

The menu was in English and French, but Jesse still didn't recognize many of the dishes.

"What do you like, Jesse?"

"I like you."

"I mean to eat."

Jesse just grinned at her and watched the blush creep over her neck and cheeks.

"You know what I mean," Odette said.

"I like steak, seafood, anything really."

"Did you see the steak section?"

"How did I miss that?"

Odette pointed to it and Jesse immediately decided on the rib eye. Odette ordered something Jesse didn't understand, but she said she loved it, so Jesse was happy. After dinner, they strolled through the neighborhood, looking at the old houses mixed in with the newer buildings.

"I love Paris," Jesse said.

"And it loves you. You have come alive in the short time you've been here."

"I really have."

They walked back to the apartment and went back to bed. When neither could move anymore, Odette broke the news that she had to get going.

"I do have to work tomorrow," she said.

"Stay the night here," Jesse said.

"I can't. I've been in the same clothes since last night."

"Oh, yeah."

"I need to go home and sleep in my lonely bed and wake up early to be at my café."

Jesse felt panic in the pit of her stomach.

"When will I see you again?"

"When would you like to?"

"Tomorrow after work?"

Odette smiled at her.

"Okay. I will bring a change of clothes and go to work Monday morning from your apartment."

"That would be wonderful. I'll come by to see you at work tomorrow."

"I'd like that."

Jesse walked Odette to her car parked in the parking lot of the café. They exchanged phone numbers and kissed like teenagers before Odette finally pushed Jesse away.

"I need to go, my Jesse."

"I know."

"I will see you tomorrow."

"Yes, you will."

CHAPTER FOURTEEN

Jesse woke late Sunday morning feeling alone without Odette. It was an odd feeling, but not a horrible one. She could still get out of bed and make coffee. She just missed Odette. She opted not to make coffee, but to hurry across the street to see her.

The café was crowded and she had to wait for a seat. She stood in the entryway and felt her heart skip a beat when she finally caught a glimpse of Odette. She looked beautiful and put together, even during the early lunch rush. Jesse wanted nothing more than to go to her and pull her in her arms. She kept watching her until Odette finally turned around and saw her. She immediately crossed the room.

"Hello, my Jesse." She hugged her and kissed both her cheeks.

"Hi there. I miss you."

"Oh, you are so sweet. I miss you, too. But I must get back to work. I'll try to come see you when you're seated."

"Sounds good."

Jesse got a table and tried to focus on her menu. She really wasn't hungry, but knew if she ordered food, it would take longer which would give her more time to watch Odette. So she ordered breakfast and sipped her coffee.

Odette finally came by her table. She rested her hand lightly on Jesse's shoulder.

"Did you sleep well?" she asked.

"I did, but I woke alone."

"I know. I did, too."

"I didn't like that."

Odette smiled at her, eyes twinkling.

"You won't have to tomorrow, remember?"

"Oh, I remember," Jesse said.

Jesse's food arrived then and Odette excused herself.

"Wait," Jesse said.

"What?"

"What time will you be over tonight?"

"Between nine and ten. I look forward to it."

"So do I."

Jesse watched her walk off and was shaking from anticipation. She couldn't wait until that night when she could hold Odette again.

After breakfast, Jesse walked up to the corner market Odette had told her about. She bought some beer and a few other items for the apartment, then wandered home.

She was feeling alone when she got there. She missed Odette fiercely, but there was more to it. She had Sara on her mind. She missed her terribly. True, she felt more alive than she had in forever. But Sara was still with her. She wondered how Odette would affect her memories of Sara.

Granted, Sara had been gone for four years, but the pain still felt like it was yesterday. Though that pain had lessened in the last week or so. So now she was left with guilt. She felt guilty that she was able to enjoy the company of another woman for more than a few hours. She felt guilty that she wanted to spend all her time with Odette. She wondered if she should talk to Odette about her feelings, but reasoned she should wait. She really wanted to see where this would go with Odette and she told herself she wasn't being untrue to Sara. Sara would want her to be happy. Isn't that what Liza had always told her?

Liza. She needed her. She sent her an e-mail, even though she knew Liza would still be asleep. It was still early morning there. She was surprised when she got a response.

It turned out Liza hadn't been able to sleep, so was up early. She responded to Jesse that she was happy for her and to keep on seeing Odette to see where it might lead.

Somehow Jesse had known that's what she would say.

Jesse called Liza.

"I bet you're happy now that I talked you into that international calling plan, huh?" Liza said.

"It's good to hear your voice, too."

Liza laughed.

"So, what's wrong, Jess? You finally found someone new who can make you happy. Are you looking for things to screw it up?"

"No. I so don't want to screw this up. But I feel guilty. I feel so guilty. Like I'm cheating on Sara."

"Jess, listen to me. Sara's gone. She's not coming back. You've had a hard time with that since the moment it happened. But you need to accept it now and move on."

Jesse was silent as she thought about what that would mean. Saying good-bye to Sara felt like the ultimate betrayal.

"I don't know if I'm ready to say good-bye to Sara."

"What happens if you don't?" Liza said.

"I don't know."

"Will Odette want to share you?"

"I don't know."

"Boy, it's a good thing you called. We need to hash this out and fast. When do you see Odette again?"

"She's coming to stay the night tonight."

"Oh goody. A sleepover."

"Liza, be serious."

"Sorry. Look, I think all this stems from the fact that you never got to say good-bye to Sara. It happened so quickly. I think it would have been easier if you could have told her good-bye and heard from her that it's okay for you to be happy."

"Maybe, but that's not the way it went down."

"No, it's not," Liza said. "Still, you have to know she'd want you to live life. You've been a shell of the person you were. And now, you're coming back to life. You're enjoying things again. And you enjoy this woman. Don't deny it, Jess. Don't deny yourself living."

"But what about Sara?"

"Sara will always be with you. She'll always be a part of your life. Just don't make her the focal point. Don't worship her like a goddess. Accept that she was your partner for years and you loved her, but she's gone now. She will live in your memory, but make a place in your heart to live in the present."

"That makes sense," Jesse said. "Thanks, Liza."

"You're welcome. So, tell me all about this wonderful woman."

"Well, I've already told you so much in my e-mails."

"I know. She's wonderful. What else?" Liza laughed.

"She's older and smart and warm and caring."

"Someone's got it bad. How much older?"

"I have no idea."

"Y'all haven't exchanged ages?"

"Not yet. But she's not much older than we are. Maybe a few years."

"And you really think you could do the long haul thing with her?"

"I don't know. I mean, I've only just met her. But something feels different about this one. Something feels…different."

"Okay. Well, that's not very descriptive, but I guess I'll take it."

"Yeah. I don't know."

"Okay. Well, I hate to cut this short but I'm gonna try to go back to bed for a while."

"Thanks for talking things through with me."

"My pleasure. Don't be a stranger over there."

"I won't."

Jesse hung up the phone feeling much better. She popped a beer and sat on her couch, pondering her next move. She had a long time before Odette got there and couldn't decide what to do with all that time on her hands. It finally hit her that she had classes the next day so opened her laptop and books and went to work on her homework.

Several hours later, she felt like she had a good handle on things and she was hungry again. She wanted to go to the café, but didn't want to look desperate. Instead, she made herself dinner, which killed another hour. She felt like time was standing still. She wanted it to hurry forward and then stand still once Odette got there. Somehow she didn't think that was going to happen.

She went for a walk around campus after dinner and got home just at nine. She hopped in the shower and was dressed when her phone rang. It was Odette.

"Hi, Jesse. I'm here."

"I'll be right out."

Jesse opened the door to see a radiant Odette standing there.

"Oh, Odette. You're finally here." She pulled her into a hug.

"I am, my Jesse. Finally. This day seemed to never end. You smell good. You are wet. You just showered?"

"I did. I went for a walk after dinner, so I thought a shower would be nice."

"May I take one?"

"Of course," Jesse said. She waited in the front room for what seemed an eternity. Finally, Odette walked out in a thick white bathrobe. Her hair was slicked back against her head and Jesse's heart skipped a beat.

"My God, you're gorgeous," she said.

"Thank you. So are you."

"I mean it. I want you right now."

Odette put her hand out and Jesse took it. She walked them into the bedroom and slowly stripped off her bathrobe.

"If you want me now, then you shall have me now."

She lay back on the bed and Jesse climbed on top. She kissed her deeply while she dragged her hand over Odette's breasts. She explored first one, then the other breast. She teased and caressed and pinched and kneaded.

Jesse kissed down Odette's neck and took a nipple in her mouth. She tasted fresh and clean and Jesse loved it. She kissed lower still until she was finally between her legs. Odette spread her legs to give Jesse easier access.

Jesse couldn't believe the flavor of Odette. She was delicious and Jesse couldn't get enough. She lapped and sucked and stroked and licked. Odette tasted so good Jesse couldn't stop moving her tongue all over her. She finally focused her attention on Odette's clit while she moved her fingers inside her. She coaxed her to one orgasm after another until finally, she was satiated for the moment.

She moved next to Odette and took her in her arms.

"I'm sorry. You must think I'm an animal."

"What is there to be sorry for?"

"I didn't even talk to you. I just had my way with you."

"Jesse, it's okay. Let's just say it took the edge off. Now we can visit, then we will love again."

Jesse nodded.

"And I for one," Odette said, "very much enjoyed that. So no need to be sorry, okay?"

"Okay."

Odette snuggled in closer to Jesse.

"I love how you feel wrapped around me," she said.

"I could say the same."

"Good."

"So, tell me, Odette. How was your day?"

"My day was good. Busy, but good. How was yours?"

"Mine was nice. Mellow, but nice."

"It was nice to see you at the café," Odette said. "It made me happy."

"I'm glad you don't think I'm pathetic, but I had to see you."

"Not pathetic, Jesse. I wanted to see you, too. And it's much easier for you to come by the café than it is for me to come here."

"I suppose that's true."

Jesse kissed Odette. It was a soft kiss, but she hoped it conveyed how special she thought she was.

"What was that for?" Odette asked.

"Because I couldn't resist."

"You are so sweet."

"How is it a woman like you is single?" Jesse asked.

"Believe it or not I am, um, guarded? Is that right?"

Jesse was surprised. Nothing about Odette indicated she was anything more than warm and open.

"You are?"

"Yes. Which is why I ask how you get to me so. And in such a short time."

"I don't know. I don't get it either. What's happening, I mean."

"You have mourned for years now. Can you stop?"

Jesse propped herself up on an elbow.

"I don't know. I talked to my best friend for a long time about that today."

"Of course, I want you to move on."

"I think I can," Jesse said.

"Good."

"Can you open up to me? Will you tell me your secrets and fears and dreams?"

"I will try, my Jesse. It won't be easy."

"If not, then what is this we have? Is it simply physical?"

"I don't want to believe that."

Jesse lay back down and took Odette in her arms. She wondered how she would feel if it was just a physical relationship. That would certainly be easier for her. It was definitely what she was used to, so she would be much more comfortable with that.

"What do you want, Jesse?"

"We've known each other for what? A week? A week and a half? I think we should see where this goes. We don't need to make any groundbreaking decisions right now."

"True."

Odette kissed Jesse, prodding her lips open with her tongue. Jesse felt her body responding. She pulled Odette closer and kissed her harder.

"You must get naked," Odette said.

Jesse stood and stripped out of her clothes. She was very much aware of Odette's focus on her every move. She found it arousing to be the subject of such scrutiny, and when she stood naked in front of Odette, she was swollen and wet and ready for her.

"Come here," Odette said. She held out her hand and Jesse took it. She lay on the bed next to Odette.

"I want you, Jesse." Odette ran her hand between her own legs. "I need you. I am so wet for you."

Jesse reached out and felt Odette's pussy. It was hot and creamy and Jesse knew she had to have her again. She slipped her fingers inside her and stroked her silky walls.

"You feel amazing," Jesse said.

"I need more. Please, Jesse. Harder. More."

Jesse was happy to oblige. She slid more fingers inside Odette and plunged in and out, until she was afraid she would hurt her.

"Oh God, yes, Jesse." Odette spread her legs wider and placed her own hand on her clit. Jesse knelt to watch Odette swallow her fingers and to watch her fingers play over herself. Jesse was close to exploding herself, but kept it together long enough to feel Odette crush her fingers as she cried out when she came.

Odette lay still as she caught her breath. Jesse lay next to her, waiting hopefully for her touch.

When Odette was ready, she ran her hand between Jesse's legs and over her clit.

"Oh, Jesse. You are so big."

Jesse bit her lip and forced herself not to come at the first contact. She wanted Odette to fuck her. Really fuck her like she'd just done to her, but didn't know how long she'd last.

Odette rubbed her clit and Jesse knew it was a losing battle. She felt the energy coalesce deep inside as the orgasm grew near. Suddenly the ball burst open and the energy shot through her body as the climax hit.

"I didn't mean to come so soon," she said.

"It's okay. I'm not through."

Jesse felt Odette's fingers exploring every inch between her legs. She spread wider, needing more.

"How do you like it Jesse? Soft and sweet or hard and fast?"

Just the sound of Odette talking to her like that made her clit harder.

"Fuck me, Odette. That's what I want."

"Oh, now you're talking. I like it when you talk to me like that."

"Yeah?" Jesse was breathing heavily. Something about carnal sex with Odette was making her hotter by the minute.

"I will fuck you, Jesse." She moved her fingers deep inside her.

Jesse had no idea how many fingers were in her, but she felt full and it felt amazing. Odette moved in and out hard and fast, driving deeper with each thrust. Jesse arched to meet each one.

While she made love to Jesse, Odette moved to straddle Jesse's leg and Jesse could feel her hard clit rubbing against her.

"Oh dear God," Jesse said.

"Mm, yes. You need more?"

"I don't know how much more I can take."

"Oh, Jesse," Odette said as she continued to move on her. "I'm going to come again."

"Yes. Please come for me."

Odette ground into her while she continued to thrust her fingers with greater vigor. The blatant wantonness of her made Jesse lightheaded. She was more aroused than she could remember.

"Jesse!" Odette cried as she came again. She rubbed her pussy all over Jesse's leg, leaving a trail of cream on her.

Jesse couldn't hold out much longer. She followed Odette's lead and began to rub her own swollen clit.

"Yes, my Jesse. Help me get you off. You are so hot inside. And so tight. I want to fuck you like this forever."

Jesse's head was spinning as she continued to rub her hard clit. It was giant in its need and she pressed it hard into her pubis. She closed her eyes and saw the light show behind her eyelids as the orgasm approached. She focused on nothing but the sensations that were flooding her body.

She finally could take no more. The lights exploded at the same time her body felt like it was being torn apart by the force of the orgasm shooting through her.

"Oh wow. Just wow," Jesse said when she could breathe again. "That was amazing."

"Yes, my Jesse. It was. I like sex with you. Last night was so special. Tonight was different, but still fun."

"Yes, it was. You're amazing."

"We are amazing together. I really like you, Jesse."

"I like you, too, Odette. I can't wait to see where this goes."

CHAPTER FIFTEEN

The next morning, Jesse woke up in a wonderful mood with Odette lying next to her. She rolled over and gazed at her, loving her naked body exposed for her pleasure. She bent over and took a nipple in her mouth, playing over the tip of it with her tongue. She teased the other with her fingers then moved her mouth to Odette's neck, where she sucked and nibbled until Odette finally stirred.

"Mm," she murmured. "That feels nice."

Jesse kissed back to her breast and sucked on her nipple again.

"That feels nicer," Odette said.

Jesse released her grip on her nipple and kissed lower, finally ending up between her legs.

"I can't get enough of you," she said as she gazed longingly at the feast in front of her.

"I'm glad. I want you to take all you want."

Jesse buried her face between Odette's legs and lapped at her. She ran her tongue over every inch of her, tasting the remnants of the previous night's lovemaking.

"You're delicious," she said.

"I'm happy you think so."

Jesse worked her tongue inside Odette and out and was rewarded when she heard her scream as the orgasm hit.

"I must taste you now," Odette said. She maneuvered between Jesse's legs and sucked her juicy lips. She moved her tongue inside, licking as deep as she could. She ran her tongue over Jesse's clit and sucked it until Jesse came.

Odette moved into Jesse's arms and they dozed again, briefly.

"What time is it?" Odette asked when they woke again.

"It's five thirty."

"I must get going. I need to open the café."

"Okay. You take a shower first. Can I come over after my shower and get a cup of coffee?"

"Sure. That would be nice."

Jesse lay in bed replaying the night before as she waited for Odette to get out of the shower. She wondered what secrets Odette harbored. She was almost resentful that she'd shared about Sara, but Odette wouldn't share with her. Then she cautioned herself that this thing they had was still young. There was time.

Odette was dressed when she came into the room.

"I'm going to leave. I'll see you in a little while?"

"Count on it." Jesse climbed out of bed and kissed Odette good-bye.

She took her shower, dressed quickly, and grabbed her back pack. She headed across the street for coffee. The sight of Odette took her breath away, even though she'd just seen her a half an hour before.

Odette brought two cups of coffee and sat with her.

"I thought you'd be too busy to join me," Jesse said.

"I got the coffee going and turned everything on in the kitchen. Now the others can take over. I have to get to my office, though, and work on my books."

"Right now?"

"No. I'll sit with you. Soon, people will talk, you know."

"How do you feel about that?"

"I don't think I'll like it."

Jesse was uncomfortable with the answer.

"Will you keep me a secret forever then?"

"I like to keep personal and work separate."

"Should I not come around as much?"

"Maybe we'll talk about this tonight," Odette said. "I'd like to come over again."

Jesse was confused. She thought she and Odette had something special, but maybe it was just fun and games to her.

"I think we should. And I'd like you to come over again."

"Good. I need to get to work. You have a good day, my Jesse."

"You, too."

Jesse finished her coffee and had a second cup, just because it was too early to get to class. She missed Odette already. The feeling was so unfamiliar to her. But she liked it and was happy. Except Odette seemed mysterious sometimes. She was looking forward to seeing her that night so they could set some ground rules.

She finished her coffee and walked to school. She focused on all her classes, determined to learn all she could to better her skill. Occasionally, thoughts of Odette would penetrate her focus, but she fought to keep herself on task.

After school, she went to the art room to work on a painting of the Paris skyline. It was coming along nicely and she was able to lose herself in her art for several hours. When she finally looked at the clock, she saw it was almost eight. She washed her brushes and hurried home to make a quick dinner.

Odette arrived shortly after nine, looking radiant, as usual.

Jesse pulled her into a hug and kissed her.

"It's good to see you," she said.

"And you."

"How was your day?" Jesse asked.

"It was long. But wonderful. Every day I do what I love. I'm very lucky."

"That's how it will be when I paint for a living."

"Yes, it will. You are very lucky, too."

"Come on in. I'll pour us some wine. We'll talk."

"I hope I didn't upset you this morning," Odette said.

"Sit. We'll talk."

Jesse poured them each a glass of wine and handed one to Odette. She sat next to her on the couch.

"You confused me," Jesse said.

"I'm sorry."

"I understand no PDA," Jesse said.

"I'm sorry. I don't understand."

"PDA…Public display of affection. I get that I can't kiss you at work. But at the park, you told me if people saw us together they would be happy for us. Now you say you're worried people will talk. I don't understand. And you tell me you like to see me at the café, but today made it seem like I'm there too much. Please explain what's going on in your head."

"I'm sorry. I don't mean to confuse you."

"So about the café. Can I go see you there or not?"

Odette was silent and Jesse felt a knot in her stomach. If she was told she couldn't see her, she would be crushed. And how had that happened? How had she let herself fall so fast?

"Jesse. I want to see you as much as you want to see me."

"But?"

"I don't know."

"Do you not want people to know you're seeing someone? Or is it me? Do I embarrass you?"

"No. Oh, no. Nothing like that."

"Then what?"

"I like when you come see me. But I can't make a habit of sitting with you or paying you special attention."

"So, no one can know about us. What if someone sees us in public?"

"That is different."

"Odette, do I make you happy?"

"Oh, yes."

"Then why can't we let people know?"

"I'm not ready Jesse. It's too soon."

"Fair enough. Should I avoid the café for a while?"

"I don't know."

"I suppose that says it all."

"Jesse, please don't be mad at me."

"I don't know that I'm mad. Just confused. I can't get enough of you. And if I see you only for a few minutes while you're working, it's better than nothing for me."

"I understand this."

"And last night you said you like it when I come by. I guess I don't like the inconsistency."

"The what?"

"The contradiction. The fact that it was okay yesterday and not today."

"I do like it when you come by. I can't help that. I like to see you, Jesse. It's true. But I realized this morning that people might start to notice and I don't want that to get in the way of my work."

"Okay. So we'll say I can still come by but you can't pay me special attention. Surely you have other regular customers."

"Okay, Jesse. We'll try that and see how it works. But I can't sit with you all the time."

"I'm not asking you to."

"Thank you for understanding."

"I'm not sure I do. But I'll try."

"Will you kiss me now, Jesse?"

Jesse wasn't much in the mood for kissing.

"Is this all physical to you, Odette? You said no last night, but I'm asking again. If it is, that's fine, but I need to know."

"It is too soon for all this seriousness, don't you think? We should be enjoying each other now only."

Jesse's mind was racing. She tried to make sense of everything Odette had said. She still didn't understand where she stood, but she did have to agree that it was early in their relationship and she should just relax and see how things played out.

"Should I leave?" Odette said.

"No," Jesse was quick to respond. "Definitely not."

"Can we talk about something else?"

"Sure. Are we going to the park Friday?"

"Of course. I wouldn't miss it."

"Good." Jesse stretched out her arm and pulled Odette close. It felt good to be holding her, she had to admit. She liked how they molded together. She kissed the top of her head.

"You smell good," she said.

"Thank you. So do you. So, tell me, how was your day?"

"It was great. Classes went well and I worked on a painting for a few hours. It was a good day."

"I want to see more of your work sometime," Odette said.

"I need to get more done. I guess there's a showing for students at the end of June and I want to have some stuff in the show."

"Oh how exciting. May I go to the showing?"

"Of course. I'd like that."

"Good." Odette looked into Jesse's eyes and Jesse saw a longing that made her boxers wet. She couldn't deny her attraction to Odette, regardless of anything else. She leaned forward and kissed her. Her lips were soft and tasted of the wine they were drinking.

"That's better," Odette said.

"Yes, it is." Jesse kissed her again, harder this time. She moved her mouth over Odette's with the need that was quickly overcoming her.

Odette opened her mouth and Jesse quickly entered her, her tongue probing and tasting every inch. They kissed for what seemed an eternity, until Odette pulled away.

"Take me to bed, Jesse. I need to make love with you."

They made their way to the bedroom and resumed kissing while they hurriedly stripped each other of their clothes. When they were naked, they fell into bed together. Their hands glided over each other, touching everywhere and exploring every spot they found.

"I must have you," Odette said.

Jesse rolled onto her back and opened her legs.

"Do you have any toys? I like toys."

"I didn't bring any with me," Jesse said. "They're all in storage back home."

"We will have to get some," Odette said. "We will go toy shopping. That will be fun."

"Yes, it will." Jesse lay spread eagle, hoping Odette would touch her soon.

Odette must have read her mind as she reached between Jesse's legs and stroked her to attention.

"I love how you respond," she said.

"I love your touch," Jesse said hoarsely.

Odette continued to play with her clit until Jesse was almost in pain. Odette slipped her fingers inside her then and filled her.

"That feels amazing," Jesse said.

"I am glad. You feel amazing, too."

Odette kept up her thrusting until Jesse teetered on the edge. She moved her hand back to Jesse's clit and rubbed it until Jesse felt the world disappearing. All that existed was the feeling of Odette. Odette was all that mattered. She finally could hold out no longer and called Odette's name as she rocketed into oblivion.

"Oh, Jesse. You were made to be loved."

"You sure know what you're doing."

Odette smiled.

"Thank you."

When Jesse had caught her breath, she kissed Odette while she moved a hand to her breast. She loved the feel of her soft skin and the contrast of her hard, puckered nipple. She closed her fingers on her nipple and twisted it slightly, eliciting a gasp of pleasure from Odette.

She kissed down her neck and closed her mouth on the other nipple. It responded quickly and she greedily sucked on it as she moved her hand lower. She found Odette's clit hard and slick and she glided easily over it. She found her opening wet and ready for her and easily slid her fingers inside.

"Oh, yes, Jesse. Yes."

Jesse kissed down Odette's belly until she could take her clit in her mouth. She flicked her tongue over it while she continued to move her fingers in and out. She felt Odette pressing the back of her head and fought to breathe as she continued to lick and suck on her.

She felt the tremors on her fingers and knew Odette was close. She sucked harder and was rewarded when Odette pushed her face into her as she came again and again.

Jesse didn't stop licking until Odette cried out one more time and then tapped her on her shoulder.

"No more, Jesse. I can't take any more right now."

Jesse kissed and sucked Odette's inner thighs, leaving little marks she knew no one would see before moving up to hold Odette.

"I might have marked your thighs," she said.

"That's okay." Odette laughed. "You'll make me feel like a schoolgirl if you did."

"I figured no one would see them."

"Just you, my Jesse."

Jesse loved when she called her that. It made all her worries and insecurities seem unnecessary.

"I do like you, Jesse. Surely you know that."

"I do. I'm sorry I got so weird earlier."

"It's okay. I guess I should tell you. I was never interested in a relationship for a long time."

"Because of your work?"

"Partly. But also because I liked different women, you know?"

"Oh my God, Odette. Are you telling me you were a player?"

"I'm sorry. I don't understand."

"You slept around. You had sex with lots of women."

"*Oui*. That is what I'm saying. Please don't think less of me."

"I don't. I was the same way."

"You? But you were mourning your partner. Surely you weren't a…what did you call it?"

"A player. Yes, I was. I felt numb, dead, in my life. Nothing made me feel alive except encounters with nameless women."

"So you understand why I am scared, I guess is a good word for it? This is new for me."

"I totally get it. But we need to be honest with each other. If one of us is too scared to go on, we need to say so."

"I like you, Jesse. I don't want to not see you. It's just this morning, my feelings came back. You know the natural way you feel when you think about relationships."

"I do know. But I don't get that feeling with you."

"I don't mostly when I'm with you. I don't know what happened this morning. I got scared."

"That's okay. Let's just promise to talk about it when we start to feel that way, okay?"

"I promise," Odette said.

"So you told me once that you had been in love. When was that?"

"It was a long time ago," Odette said.

"And? What happened? How long were you together?"

"We were together ten years."

"Wow! That's impressive."

"Yes. We were the perfect couple. Everyone said."

"So what happened?" Jesse asked again.

"She cheated on me."

Jesse felt the heat boil inside her. How dare someone cheat on Odette? How could they?

"She was a fool."

"I vowed never to care again."

"I don't blame you."

"So I am, um, weary, Jesse."

Jesse knew she meant wary, but didn't correct her.

"I don't blame you," she said again. "I'm not going to hurt you, Odette."

"Somehow I trust you. And this is scary."

"Trust is very scary. But I trust you won't hurt me, either."

"Not on purpose, my Jesse. Never on purpose."

Jesse pulled Odette close and held her. So, she was a player, too. Jesse hadn't even considered that. But that worked. They could understand each other's fears. It wasn't a bad thing.

She kissed Odette and ran her hand down her body.

"Are you sure you're through for the night?"

"I'm sure of nothing right now."

Jesse moved her hand between Odette's legs. She was wet and warm.

"You always feel so inviting," Jesse said.

"I always invite you in."

"Good."

Jesse kissed her again and lightly traced her opening with her fingers.

"Jesse, please. Don't tease me."

"But teasing can be fun."

"I need you."

Jesse dipped her fingertips just inside Odette. She pulled them out again.

"No fair," Odette said.

Jesse laughed and allowed her fingers to slide a little further in before pulling them out.

"I'm going to take care of myself if you don't stop teasing me."

As tempting as that was to watch Odette please herself, Jesse wanted to be the one to make her come. She buried her fingers as deep as they would go and slowly withdrew them. She did this several times before Odette was digging her fingernails into her back.

Jesse finally moved her fingers to Odette's clit and rubbed there until Odette threw her head back and screamed as she climaxed.

"You are so much fun," Jesse said.

"So are you. But my Jesse, we must get some sleep. The morning will be here soon. Hold me, please."

Jesse stretched out her arms and Odette scooted into them, once again a perfect fit. Jesse held her tight as she fell into a deep sleep.

CHAPTER SIXTEEN

Jesse and Odette settled into an easy routine over the next several weeks. Jesse usually started her day with coffee at the café and Odette no longer told her not to come by. She'd then attend her classes and work late into the evening on art projects for the upcoming show. Nights were spent in her tiny apartment with Odette. They had even gotten Odette her own passcard for the front door.

Jesse was happier than she'd been in years. She still felt guilty on occasion, but talks with Liza usually helped her through it. And the nights with Odette were wonderful.

She was doing well in her classes, though she thought she could do better. So she pushed herself harder to study and practice more. She had several paintings completed by mid-June and was still working on sketches, so she would have a decent amount for the student's show. She missed having Liza's constant feedback. Odette would comment on the sketches in the apartment, but hadn't seen any paintings yet. Still, Jesse was confident they were good. And the feedback she got from her instructors was encouraging, at least.

One warm Friday evening, she walked into the café shortly after the dinner rush had ended. Technically, she wasn't supposed to meet Odette until eight for their weekly trip to the park, but she was tired of painting and just wanted to see Odette.

She took a seat at an open table and waited until Giselle came over to take her order. She ordered an ice cream sundae and then sat back as she looked around for Odette. Odette saw her and hurried over.

"You're early," she said.

"I was jonesin' for some ice cream."

"I'm sorry?"

"I had a craving."

"Oh." Odette laughed. "I have a craving, too, but not for ice cream."

"I hope to satisfy that craving later," Jesse said.

"I'm sure you will. Let me finish up and I'll join you."

Jesse smiled at the unexpected treat. Odette got back just as her ice cream was served. They shared the sundae in happy silence.

"Are you ready to go?" Jesse asked when they finished.

"I am. Let me grab the wine and the blanket."

They walked hand in hand to the park where pop music was playing. Jesse felt young at heart listening to it.

"This is not my thing," Odette said as they sat on the blanket.

The statement made Jesse wonder how old Odette was. She'd wondered before, but never asked. Tonight she was more than curious.

"Would you rather leave?"

"Would you be disappointed? Let's go get some dinner."

Jesse thought of the ice cream they'd just shared, but thought a restaurant with Odette would be nice. They packed everything into Odette's bag and walked farther up the street. They came to a sidewalk café.

"This looks perfect," Odette said.

They waited to be seated, and Jesse thought Odette had never looked better. She was wearing a multi-colored calf length skirt and a white peasant blouse. She pulled her to her and resisted the urge to kiss her. Though she left her arm draped around her waist.

They got a small table on the patio and enjoyed a wonderful sunset as they sipped their drinks. Jesse couldn't begin to pronounce what Odette had ordered for her, but the pasta with clams in a white wine sauce was delicious. They were full and relaxed as they sauntered back to Jesse's apartment.

"Just out of curiosity, who takes care of your house while you're here?" Jesse finally asked.

"My adult daughter lives with me."

"Doesn't she wonder where you are?"

"She knows."

"She knows?" Jesse couldn't wipe the smile from her face. "About us?"

"Of course. Madeline knows everything that happens in my world."

"How old is Madeline?"

"She is thirty. She got out of a breakup a few years ago and has been living with me since. It's nice."

"Thirty?" Jesse tried to do some math in her head. "You must have had her awfully young."

"Ah, my Jesse. You are so sweet."

Jesse wanted to ask how old she'd been. She wanted to ask how old she was now. But she figured Odette would tell her when she was ready.

"Actually," Odette said. "Madeline would like to meet you."

"She would?" Jesse felt the immediate fear that came with the subject of meeting someone's family. She mentally calmed herself. It would be awesome to meet Odette's daughter.

"Yes, she would. We were hoping you'd come over for dinner tomorrow night."

"Do you work tomorrow?"

"No. I took the day off again. I like lazy Saturdays with you. So we can go over early in the day and make an evening of it."

"That sounds great. What should I bring?"

"Your hot self. Seriously, Madeline will have done all the shopping. She and I will cook for you."

"I can't complain about that. Still, I feel bad showing up empty handed. Maybe I'll bring some wine."

"You'll be with me, so you won't be arriving at our house alone. You don't need to bring anything. We'll have wine and beer. It'll be fine."

"If you say so."

"I say so. Now, tomorrow is a big day. Let's get some rest."

They got to the bedroom and rest was the last thing either wanted. Jesse kissed Odette possessively, crushing their mouths together. She put all her passion into that kiss, leaving no doubt the mood she was in.

Odette kissed her back with equal passion and wrapped her arms and legs around her. Jesse ground her pelvis into her, pressing into her wet center. The feel of her creaminess made her passion surge.

She pulled back enough to run her fingers between Odette's legs. She slid them easily inside while she caressed her clit with her thumb.

"Oh, Jesse. It's too soon."

"Come for me, baby."

"Oh, Jesse!" Odette came on Jesse's hand in no time at all.

"You were ready," Jesse said.

"I'm always ready for you."

"I'm glad."

Jesse began moving her fingers inside Odette again and didn't stop until Odette climaxed again and again.

When Odette couldn't take any more, Jesse rolled over and pulled her close.

"Oh, no," Odette said. "Not yet."

She kissed Jesse with all the energy she could muster. She moved down her body and took a pink nipple in her mouth. She drew it in deep and Jesse squirmed at the feelings flooding her body. Her nipple was wired directly to her clit, which was already rock hard from loving Odette.

Odette kissed her way down to where Jesse's legs met.

"What have we here?" She asked before she licked her clit. "You are so big for me."

"I want you, Odette."

"I am glad."

Odette licked and sucked on Jesse's clit until Jesse felt her whole body tense. She held her breath as Odette worked until the orgasm finally tore through her body, leaving her limp and relaxed.

"You are so good at that," she said.

"Thank you. You're not so bad yourself."

Jesse smiled as she held Odette and fell asleep.

They woke the next morning and picked up where they'd left off the night before. Jesse loved Odette's body and couldn't get enough of it. She was teasing her nipples before Odette was even fully awake.

"Good morning," Odette said.

"Mm hm."

"You're frisky this morning."

"I am. I want you all the time, Odette."

"That's good because I always want you, too."

Jesse climbed between Odette's legs and savored the flavor that was hers and hers alone. She licked and sucked and devoured everything she could get her mouth on. And when she needed more, she added her fingers to the mix, feeling deep inside her while she continued to lick and suck on her. She glanced up and saw Odette tweaking her nipples, which made her desire to please her triple. She worked frantically, plunging her fingers deep and sucking hard until she felt Odette's hand behind her head, pressing her face into her.

Odette was moving against her and she could barely breathe. But it didn't matter. All that mattered was the scream Odette let out a few moments later when she finally found her release.

They showered and got ready for their day. They went to the *marche* and bought some food and Jesse convinced Odette to at least let her bring flowers to dinner that night. They walked to the flower stand where Jesse was greeted warmly by Amelie.

"Jesse!" She hugged her and kissed both her cheeks. "So good to see you again."

Jesse felt a little uncomfortable, but shook it off and hugged her back.

"And who is your friend?" Amelie said.

"This is Odette. Odette, this is Amelie."

"So nice to meet you," Odette took her hand in both of her own.

"And you. How can I help you today?" Amelie said.

"We need flowers for a dinner tonight," Jesse said, then turned to Odette. "I've no idea what colors."

"How about different colors?" Odette said. "I want a bouquet of bright, bright flowers. Lots of different colors."

"I can do that," Amelie said.

Jesse watched as they chose flowers and put together a beautiful bunch. She loved to watch Odette do anything, even interact with Amelie. It made her smile.

When Odette walked over to Jesse with the bouquet, Jesse pulled out her wallet.

"How much?"

"Those are, how you say, on me?"

"Oh no," Jesse said. "That wouldn't be right."

"Yes, it is. Beautiful flowers for a beautiful woman. It is my treat."

"Well, thank you," Jesse said.

"You are welcome. You two go. Enjoy the day. Spread the sunshine with your happiness."

As they walked off, Odette took Jesse's hand in her free hand. "How well do you know her?"

"Who?"

"You know who. Did you sleep with her?"

Jesse thought about denying it, but didn't want to lie. After all, she was sure she'd run into people Odette had been with. Maybe she already had. She didn't want to think about it.

"Yes," she finally said. "We had a night."

"Tell me."

"What?"

"How did you end up with her?"

"She asked me out. We went to dinner and then dancing. Then went back to my place. Not a lot to tell."

"I remember you the next morning. You were tired."

"I was. I'm sorry, Odette. I guess I wasn't thinking when I suggested we pick up some flowers."

"I am not jealous. It was before us. I just wondered. And please don't be sorry. The flowers are beautiful."

They went home and put everything away.

"What shall we do now?" Jesse pulled Odette into her arms, craving more of her.

"We shall go to my house." She kissed Jesse then stepped out of her embrace.

"You sure we don't need a nap first?"

"Quite. Come on. Let's go."

They crossed the street to the café parking lot to Odette's car.

"How are you?" Odette said.

"I'm a little nervous." Jesse said. She didn't want to point out she was probably closer to Odette's daughter's age than to Odette, but the thought wouldn't stay out of her mind. She hoped Madeline wouldn't judge her as being too young for her mother.

"Don't be."

"Meeting family always does that to me."

"Well, Madeline is looking forward to meeting you and I think it's important you two know each other. So relax, my sweet Jesse."

Jesse watched as they left the Latin Quarter and drove to a nearby section.

"This section of Paris has the oldest neighborhood in Paris," Odette said. "It is La Marais. It's also the gay area. So, it's a good mix. My neighborhood is nice."

"You live this close to work?" Jesse said.

"I do."

They pulled up in front of an old renaissance building.

"This is where my apartment is." Odette said. She drove around the block and under the building to park.

"What a beautiful area," Jesse said.

"Yes. We will explore it next Saturday," Odette said. "Now, come."

She took Jesse's hand and led her inside the building to the elevators. They got on, and as soon as the door closed behind them, Odette was pressed against Jesse.

"Let's make out like kids," she said.

Jesse pulled her close and kissed her. Odette opened her mouth and let Jesse slide her tongue inside. Jesse pulled her tighter and was so lost in the kiss, it didn't register that the doors had opened.

"We are here," Odette announced.

They crossed the hall and opened the door. The smells that greeted Jesse were wonderful and dinner wasn't for several more hours. Her stomach growled loudly.

"We must get you some food," Odette said. She led Jesse through the entry hall and into a large, spacious living room. It was a white room with lots of color. The carpet and couches and chairs were white, but the colorful paintings on the wall brought the room to life.

"I love what you've done with this room," Jesse said.

"Thank you. I'm quite fond of it."

She took Jesse down the hall and to the kitchen, where they found Madeline working over the stove.

"Madeline dear, we're here."

Madeline didn't seem to hear and it was then Jesse saw the ear buds in her ears. She smiled. Madeline turned and started to see them. She took the ear buds out.

"I'm sorry. I was um, rocking out."

"I swear. That child and her music," Odette said. She grabbed Jesse's hand. "Madeline, this is Jesse. Jesse, Madeline."

"It's so nice to finally meet you," Madeline said as she came around the island and gave Jesse a big hug. "I've heard so much about you."

"It's nice to meet you, too." Jesse didn't bother to tell her she hadn't even known she existed until the day before.

"I'll be out of the kitchen in a short time. *Maman* can give you a tour and then I'll join you."

"Whatever you're cooking smells amazing."

"Thank you. I hope it'll taste as good as it smells."

"Come on, Jesse," Odette said. "Let me show you around."

She took her down the hallway and showed her the guest room and Madeline's room and then, at the end of the hall, the master suite.

Jesse took in the large room with the sliding glass doors leading to a balcony. She fell in love with the king-sized oak canopy bed draped with rust colored curtains. It was a far cry from the double bed they shared at her apartment.

"Nice bed," Jesse said.

"That's all you noticed? Why am I not surprised?" Odette laughed.

"I noticed other things, too. The beautiful dresser, the loveseat, the bed…"

"My Jesse is all about the bed. Perhaps we'll stay here tonight and enjoy it."

"I'd like that very much."

Madeline joined them and Jesse felt like a kid caught with her hand in the candy jar. Madeline didn't seem to notice, though.

"You haven't seen the best part," she said.

"There's more?" Jesse was impressed.

They walked back to the kitchen, but instead of turning right to the living room, they turned left into a beautiful sunroom. It was large and sunny and furnished with lamps and a desk with a computer on it. The rest of the room was filled with all sorts of plants and flowers.

"This is amazing," Jesse said.

"Isn't it?" Madeline said.

"This room is her baby," Odette said.

"It really is something," Jesse said. "I'd love to set up an art room in here. It would be perfect."

"I like to write poetry," Madeline said. "I love writing in this room."

"Oh, I'm sure."

"Okay," Odette said. "Well, you've seen where I live now. What do you think?"

"I'm impressed," Jesse said. "This is a nice place."

"Thank you," Odette said. "It's home."

"I can't believe you stay at my place all the time with this waiting for you."

"Maybe we can start trading. Here sometimes. Your place sometimes. But your place is so, um, convenient."

"Yes. That it is."

"If we stay here, we have less time for…sleep."

Jesse blushed.

"Oh my God, *Mére*. I'm right here," Madeline said.

"Sorry," Odette laughed. "I am human, my daughter."

"And I'm your daughter. I don't need to hear about those things."

"I said sleep," Odette said.

"But you meant other things."

Jesse was decidedly uncomfortable.

"Odette mentioned something about there being beer here?"

"Forgive our manners," Madeline said. "Yes, come."

Jesse took Odette's hand and followed Madeline to the kitchen, where she pulled two beers out of the fridge. Jesse couldn't begin to pronounce the name of them.

"These are very strong," Madeline said. She handed one to Jesse. "*Santè*."

Jesse looked questioningly at Odette.

"It means cheers," Odette said.

"Cheers," Jesse said and took a swig of the powerful ale. "Oh my God, that's good stuff. But where's yours, babe?"

"I don't drink beer."

"Well, would you like a glass of wine?"

"I'd love a glass of wine."

They drank and chatted and Jesse was surprised at how at ease Madeline seemed to be with her and how comfortable she was with Madeline. It could have been the beers. She had definitely caught a buzz.

Dinner was finally served and it was delicious, with more dishes Jesse didn't understand, but absolutely loved.

"You're quite a cook," she said.

"I learned from the best. My mom is fantastic in the kitchen."

"True," Jesse said. Odette had cooked for her on several occasions and each time was quite tasty.

Jesse did the dishes while Madeline dried and Odette relaxed at the bar and watched them. With the dishes done, Jesse stood behind Odette and nuzzled her neck.

"Mm, that feels wonderful," Odette said.

"That tastes wonderful," Jesse said.

"If you'll excuse me," Madeline said. "I am meeting some friends tonight, so must get going. It was wonderful meeting you."

"It was great meeting you, too. Thank you for having me over."

"My pleasure."

Jesse watched Madeline disappear down the hallway and turned her attention to Odette.

CHAPTER SEVENTEEN

With Madeline out of sight, Jesse turned Odette around and captured her lips. The dinner, beer and promise of love in a king-sized bed had Jesse feeling the need in a powerful way. She was definitely in the mood for Odette and didn't want to wait any longer.

"We should at least wait until Madeline is gone before we go to the bedroom," Odette said.

"That's fair. But know I want you now."

"And I want you, my Jesse."

They kissed some more and Madeline returned.

"I hate to interrupt," she said, "But I'm saying good night."

Jesse pulled away from Odette, embarrassed.

"Good night, Madeline."

"Have fun," Odette said.

"You, too," Madeline said. "Though I don't think there's much doubt you will."

As soon as she heard the door close, Jesse pulled Odette to her feet.

"I need you now."

"Take me, Jesse."

Jesse kissed Odette and ran her hand over her soft breast. Even through her clothes, the breast felt inviting. She felt her nipple harden and teased over it.

"Oh, Jesse. What you do to me."

Jesse closed her hand over Odette's breast.

"Let's get to your room," Jesse whispered.

Odette took her hand and led her to her room. Jesse was once again in awe at the size of the room and particularly the bed.

She eased Odette onto the bed and climbed on top of her. She kissed her hard on her mouth before moving it lower, down her neck to her exposed chest.

"God, I love you," Jesse said.

Odette put her hands on Jesse's shoulders and pushed her away. "What did you say?"

"Huh?" Jesse felt her gut tighten as she realized what she'd said. "I'm sorry. Did I just blow it?"

"No. But I think we need to talk about it."

Jesse's libido was quickly waning. She didn't want to talk. She didn't want to think about what she'd said. She rolled off Odette and lay on her back, staring up at the cover of the bed.

"Fine. We'll talk."

"Well, Jesse, it was a big statement."

"I suppose it was."

"Did you mean it? Or was it the heat of the moment?"

That was a good question. Jesse pondered it. First she tried to reason how she should answer it. She finally realized it wouldn't be fair to say what she thought Odette wanted to hear. She had to be honest. So, what was the answer?

"I think I meant it, Odette. I'm falling in love with you."

"I like that, Jesse. That makes me happy."

"Yeah?"

"*Oui.* I am falling in love with you, too."

Jesse's heart soared. Odette loved her. Her libido was back in full force.

"Now get me out of these clothes," Odette said.

Jesse was happy to oblige. She took Odette's shirt off and deftly unhooked her bra. She bent to take a breast in her mouth. She loved the feel of the soft flesh and sucked more deep inside her mouth. She ran her tongue over her hard nipple and savored each lick.

She ran her hand up under Odette's skirt and felt her damp panties.

"Oh, you're so wet already," Jesse said.

"Please. Let's get naked."

"I want to take you like this."

"How you tease me."

Jesse focused her attention back on Odette's breast while she slid the crotch of her panties aside and ran her fingers over her. She slid them inside and finally realized the panties had to go.

She slipped them off then moved her fingers back inside, this time easily getting as deep as she wanted. She moved her mouth to Odette's other breast while she stroked deep inside her. Odette moved against her and cried out when Jesse expertly took her to her climax.

Odette moved Jesse out of the way and stripped off her skirt.

"Your turn. Get out of those clothes," she said.

Jesse stood and quickly stripped. She climbed into bed and pulled Odette close, relishing anew the feel of their skin together. They kissed and rubbed against each other, fueling Jesse's fire. She was ready to have Odette again when Odette told her to lie on her back.

Jesse did as she was instructed and was confused when Odette got out of bed.

"Where are you going?"

"Don't you worry. You just lay there."

Jesse watched as Odette walked over to her dresser.

"Are you sure you meant what you said before, my Jesse?"

"Heck yeah. Why?"

"If you love me, you trust me, no?"

"Of course I trust you, Odette." Jesse was growing more curious by the moment. When Odette turned holding scarves, she had a better idea of what was happening.

"Are you serious?" she asked.

"You know what I'm going to do?" Odette said.

"I think so."

"Have you been tied up before?"

"No." Jesse said. She was always open to new ideas and if this is what Odette wanted, she was fine with it.

Odette took one of Jesse's feet and lightly stroked it before tying a scarf around it.

"You do not mind, do you?"

"Not if it's what you want."

"I like that, Jesse. It is what I want. Very much."

She tied the other end of the scarf around the bedpost before moving to her other foot. Soon, Jesse lay forced spread eagle on the bed. She liked being open and on display for Odette. It aroused her more than she thought it would.

Odette moved to the head of the bed and tied Jesse's hand to the post, then moved to the other side and did the same.

"How do you feel?" Odette asked.

"Aroused," Jesse said.

"Good," Odette said. "I am aroused, too. Very much so."

She reached between her own legs and coated her fingers with her juices, then ran them over Jesse's lips.

"Do you taste how aroused I am?"

"You're delicious," Jesse said. She tried to suck Odette's fingers, but Odette pulled them away.

"You'll have to wait for any more," she said.

Something about Odette being stern in her French accent made Jesse even hotter for her. She couldn't wait to see what she had in mind.

Odette lightly dragged her fingertips down Jesse's body, from her neck to just above her mons. Jesse shivered at the touch.

"Oh, Jesse. You are so sensitive. Look at how your nipples poke out for me."

"Your touch drives me wild."

"Good. This is very good."

Odette flattened out her hand and again dragged it the length of Jesse's body. Jesse arched to urge her hand lower, but again it stopped just above her mons.

"My Jesse wants me," Odette said.

"Desperately."

"Patience, my love."

Jesse tried to be patient, but she needed Odette with every ounce of her being. It made her crazy to be teased so. She was open and available and just wanted Odette to take her. But Odette seemed to have other plans.

She watched Odette walk back to the dresser and come back with a purple vibrator. She turned it on and stood next to the bed again. She dipped the tip of the toy inside herself, then slipped it into Jesse's mouth.

Jesse sucked greedily on the vibrator, licking every drop of Odette off it before Odette pulled it from her mouth. She turned it on and ran it over Jesse's nipples, which were already so hard they hurt. The buzzing against them sent the currents flowing to the nerve center between her legs and she bit her lip to keep from begging for release.

"Does that feel good, my Jesse?"

"Oh, God, yes."

"Good. I want to make you feel good."

"You're doing a great job of it."

Odette moved the toy away from her and replaced it with her mouth. She drew a nipple in deep while she placed the toy between Jesse's legs.

"Oh God, please," Jesse moaned.

Odette released her grip on Jesse's nipple and stood so she could see between her legs.

"I love how much you swell for me," she said.

"I feel like I'm going to burst," Jesse said.

"You look like it."

Odette pressed the vibrator's tip into Jesse's clit. That's all it took for Jesse to finally let go and soared into oblivion, lost on the waves of the orgasm. When she came back to reality, Odette was untying her legs.

"That was fun, Jesse."

"Yeah, it was."

"How did you feel? Vulnerable? Ashamed? Anything?"

"Not ashamed. Not with you. Never with you. I suppose I felt a little vulnerable, but I trusted you."

"Trust is important, Jesse."

"It is. And it's a two-way street."

"I trust you."

"I'm glad. I'll never betray that trust."

Once she was untied, Jesse made love to Odette again. It was slow and deliberate. She took her time, once again exploring every inch of her like she did their first time together. Something had shifted that night. There was a connection there stronger than before. It was real and she felt it and hoped Odette did, too.

When they were satiated, Jesse held Odette and they drifted off to sleep. At some point in the middle of the night, Jesse woke up and Odette wasn't against her. It was then she remembered she was in a king-size bed and she moved over until she found Odette and wrapped her close to herself again.

They woke early and made love until Odette announced they had to get going. She needed to get to work. They took a shower together, where Jesse lathered Odette up. She turned Odette so she faced the wall and reached between her legs from behind. She dropped the loofah and used her fingers, rubbing her swollen clit. She felt Odette collapse back against her as she came and she held her up, happy to have brought her to another climax.

"You don't stop, do you, my Jesse?"

"Not if I don't have to."

They got out of the shower and dressed quickly, as Odette was worried she'd be late to open the café. When they got to the parking lot, they kissed good-bye and Jesse watched Odette get safely inside before turning to walk across the street to her apartment.

Jesse went back to bed for a few hours and woke missing Odette. She showered and went across the street for breakfast.

Odette came over to her table.

"I'm sorry, but I'm very busy today," she said.

"It's okay. I wanted to ask you something, though."

"What is it?"

"Would it be okay if I went to check out La Marais today?"

"Of course. I'd love you to see my neighborhood. We'll go next weekend, too, but you can go today. Why even ask?"

"I just wanted to make sure it was okay with you."

"You are so sweet, my Jesse. It is fine with me."

"Good. I thought I'd take a sketch pad and capture some of it."

"I think that's an excellent idea. I need to get back to work. I'll see you tonight."

Jesse caught the train to La Marais and felt the pulse of life that beat there. She walked through the neighborhood and stopped at one of the bars for a beer. The place felt alive and vibrant. She had another beer, sure she was butchering the name of the beer Madeline had served her the day before. She stepped into the street and sat on a bench, sketching the buildings she sat in front of.

The people were a mix, as well. Tourists mingled with natives as they walked through the shops and into the bars. It felt welcoming and comfortable and Jesse hoped she was doing it justice in her drawing. She sat out in the warm sunshine for several hours before deciding to check out the Ile St. Louis and the Ile de la Cité, the oldest parts of Paris.

She fell in love with the district and was sorry she hadn't checked it out more when she had been there to see Notre Dame. She walked through the pedestrian section, along the cobblestone street. She stopped at a pub along the way for a beer before continuing her adventure to explore the medieval buildings in the area.

Jesse was glad she brought her sketch pad. There was so much to see that she'd never seen in the States. It was like a whole new world to her. She drew like a possessed woman and finally had several sketches she was happy with.

She caught the train back home in time to relax before Odette came over. When she got there, Jesse was suddenly very aware of her sparse accommodations.

"I feel bad that you spend so much time here," she said.

"What do you mean? You don't want me here as much?"

"Oh no. That's not what I meant at all. I just mean, you have such a nice place to live and these quarters are so cramped."

"I don't understand."

"It's so tight and small here."

"Ah yes, but, Jesse, how much room do we need?"

"It was so nice sharing that big bed with you last night."

"Yes, it was. And we'll go there more now. But your place is fine. It's where we first made love and I love it here."

"Well, I wish I had more to offer you."

"It is student's quarters. I understand. Tell me about your house back in the States."

"It's nice. It's your typical American ranch style home. Big enough, but not overly so. It has a living room and a sunroom, too. I do my art in the sunroom. I used to do it in an outbuilding, but then quit."

"And you quit because?"

"I quit my art all together when Sara died." Jesse felt odd talking about Sara with Odette. It was different before they were an item, but she felt strange now.

"Do you miss her still?" Odette asked.

"I do." Jesse was honest. "I mean, she's not all I think about. You are. But I do miss her still."

"That's natural, Jesse. I don't want you to feel like I'm trying to take her place. She was someone very special in your life."

"And now you are. Someone special in my life, I mean."

"Thank you, Jesse. You are very special in my life, too."

Jesse pulled Odette to her and kissed her.

"I love you so much."

"I love you, too."

They made love that night, slowly, in no hurry. They took their time, savoring every bit of each other. They finally fell asleep in the small double bed, where there was nowhere to go but each other's arms.

Chapter Eighteen

The next few weeks flew by in a blur for Jesse. She was finishing projects and selecting her favorites for the show. She was working with her instructors to learn how best to display her work using lighting to her advantage. She put her all into it, hoping to make a name for herself at the show.

She often got to the apartment minutes before Odette got there. One night, just days before the show, she met Odette at the front door.

"You're just getting home?" Odette said.

"I am. Come on in."

"I'm worried about you, my Jesse. You are working too hard,"

"It's temporary, baby. Once the show is over, I'll have much more down time."

"I hope so. I worry so much about you right now. You look exhausted."

"Thanks." Jesse laughed.

"I didn't mean to be rude. But you do look so tired. Maybe we should just sleep tonight."

"Not a chance, love. I can't say no to you."

"Ah, but I can say no to you. You need your rest. Come on. Let's lay down."

They were in the bedroom and Jesse tried to pull Odette on top of her.

"Oh no, Jesse. You lie on your stomach."

Jesse did as she was told and felt sheer pleasure at the touch of Odette's hands on her shoulders. She rubbed her lightly at first, then with more pressure. She pressed into her shoulder blades and down her back, then back to her shoulders. Jesse fought to stay awake but soon, the feel of Odette's ministrations along with her exhaustion combined to coax her into a deep sleep.

The next morning, Jesse made up for falling asleep by loving Odette fiercely. It was her favorite way to start her day. She followed Odette to the café for some coffee before heading to school. She promised Odette to take it easy. It was Friday and the show was Saturday night. She was ready.

"I will leave work early tonight," Odette said. "We'll go out for dinner."

"That would be nice," Jesse said. "I look forward to that."

Jesse's day was much easier. Everything was ready for the show. It was just a matter of showing up for the show Saturday night. She was a bundle of nerves already and it was still a day away.

Her classes were all laid back. They mostly instructed the students to be calm and have fun. Jesse tried to take their advice to heart, but it wasn't easy. She wanted to do so well, she could taste it.

She finished classes and went back to the café to see how Odette was doing. Odette came over to see her.

"How was your day?" Odette asked.

"It was very easy. Nothing going on at all."

"How are you doing?"

"I'm a nervous wreck." Jesse laughed.

"Well, I'll bring you a beer and then just give me a few minutes and we'll go get dinner."

"Sounds wonderful. Thank you."

Jesse sipped her beer and pondered the source of her nervousness. She'd been in an art show before, so it wasn't like it was her first one. Yet she was completely stressed out.

Odette came back to the table.

"Are you ready to get going?"

"I am," Jesse said.

"I thought we'd go back to the sidewalk café up the street. Is this okay?"

"That would be great."

"I wish you'd relax."

"I'm trying," Jesse said. "I think it's because I know the people I'm in the show with. The first show I did, I didn't know anyone else. Does that make sense?"

"Perfect. But you are better than the rest, my Jesse. I have faith in you."

"Thank you, Odette. I don't know what I'd do without you."

"That's not something you need to worry about. I'm right here with you."

They ate their dinner and had wine and Jesse finally began to unwind.

"It's not a big deal, right? It'll be the first of many shows I'm in."

"Yes, it is. You'll be fine when you get there tomorrow night. You just have, um, jitters."

"True."

"I'll be so proud to be with you."

"Thank you. I'll be happy to have you with me," Jesse said.

"I look forward to seeing my woman's paintings."

"I hope you'll like them. I hope they're good enough."

"I'm sure I'll love them, Jesse. I'm sure they're beautiful."

They finished their dinner and wandered through the neighborhood before making their way back to the apartment. They walked in and Jesse took Odette in her arms.

"I love you and am so glad you'll be with me tomorrow night."

"There's nowhere I'd rather be. Did I mention Madeline might stop by?"

"No. That would be great. I'd love to see her again."

"Well, we have no art show for another twenty-four hours. What do you suppose we should do?"

"I have a good idea," Jesse said. She pulled Odette closer and claimed her mouth in a passionate kiss. "I'll never get tired of kissing you."

"I like to hear this."

They kissed again before Jesse took Odette's hand and led her down the hall to her room where she made love to her for hours. She pleased her over and over again, not able to get enough of Odette's body. She used her mouth and her hands and Odette came more times than they could count.

When Odette could take no more, Jesse held her limp form and they passed out until the morning. The sun was high when Jesse opened her eyes to find her bed empty, but the smell of bacon and coffee hung on the air.

She pulled on her boxers and undershirt and padded out to the kitchen to find Odette busily making croissants to go with the bacon she'd already made.

"Babe," Jesse said. "This isn't necessary. I should be cooking for you."

"My love, you cooked for me all night last night." She blushed. "It's the least I could do to make breakfast."

Jesse's stomach growled, right on cue.

"See? You worked up an appetite. Now sit. I'll make eggs."

Jesse sat and watched Odette work in her kitchen. It didn't matter what she was doing or where she was doing it, Odette was sexy as hell. Odette served up breakfast and they enjoyed their meal together.

When it was over, they did the dishes together, then Odette sidled next to Jesse. She slipped a hand inside her boxers.

"What is this I've found?"

Jesse groaned at the contact.

"Mm. My Jesse is always so ready for me."

She dipped her fingers inside and Jesse rocked against them.

"Oh God, you feel good," Jesse said.

"So do you."

"I'm going to come."

"Do it. Come for me."

Jesse held on to Odette as her orgasm ricocheted through her body. When it stopped, she eased herself down onto a chair.

"I don't trust my legs right now," she said.

Odette smiled.

"I love making love with you."

"It's the best," Jesse said.

They spent the rest of the morning and much of the afternoon in bed, taking turns pleasing each other until they were both spent. They napped, then took their showers and made an early dinner.

Finally, it was time to get ready for the show. Jesse put on beige slacks and a purple button down shirt with a skinny tie. Odette wore a long skirt and a tight white blouse.

"You look stunning," Jesse said. "You take my breath away."

"You look quite handsome. The ladies will love you."

"I only want one lady loving me."

"And that you have," Odette said.

They walked to the art department at school and made their way to Jesse's spot in the large auditorium. She went to her locker and pulled out her paintings and set them out on easels that had been provided. She also set up her sketches and was very happy with the way she had everything positioned.

"What do you think?" Jesse asked.

"I think you do amazing work, my Jesse. I had no idea how talented you truly are."

"Thank you. That's very nice of you to say."

"I mean it. These are breathtaking."

They wandered around checking out the other students' works before it was time to take their place for the show to begin.

"Your work is much better than the rest," Odette said.

"Thank you. I don't think so, but I'm glad you do."

"I really do."

Slowly but surely, people started making their way in, browsing through the dozens of displays. People slowed at Jesse's exhibit, but it was some time before they finally had a serious nibble.

"You do good work," a man with a heavy German accent said. "I like your brushwork. I want to purchase this."

He pointed to a seascape.

Jesse got out her Square that Liza had bought for her and rang the man up. She wrapped the painting for him and watched as he left.

Odette hugged her.

"Yeah. Your first sale in Europe."

"Yep." Jesse was beaming. "That felt pretty good."

"I knew you'd be a success." A voice behind her said. She turned to see Constance standing behind them.

"Constance. What a treat." She greeted her with a big hug. "It's so good to see you."

"It's wonderful to see you, too. And to see your work. You've already improved. I can see it."

"Thanks."

Jesse put her arm around Odette and brought her forward to say hello.

"Odette," Constance said.

"Hello, Constance."

There was a definite chill in the air and Jesse wondered what had passed between the two women to make them so cold to each other.

"That's right. You two know each other." Jesse tried to act nonchalant.

"Yes," they said in unison.

Another potential buyer walked up and motioned to a sketching of Notre Dame.

"This is very nice," she said.

"Thank you."

Jesse took it off the easel and handed it to her.

"I must have this," the woman said.

Jesse rung her up and turned back to Odette and Constance. The tension was palpable.

"Is everything okay here?"

"Everything is fine, Jesse," Constance said. "I'm happy I got to see you. Maybe we'll get together. I'm in town for a week."

"I'd like that," Jesse said.

"Very good. I'll call you."

They said their good-byes and Jesse turned to Odette.

"So what was that all about?"

"Now's not the time," Odette said. "You concentrate on your show."

"I'll try," Jesse said.

The show went on, with Jesse more focused on Odette and Constance than the show, but she did her best. She sold five more paintings and a dozen sketches. It felt good to get the sales and some recognition, but also to have some money in her pocket.

When the show ended, Jesse and Odette loaded the remaining things in her storage locker.

"We should go somewhere to celebrate. Perhaps have some champagne."

"That would be great," Jesse said.

They found a restaurant on the other side of the academy and ordered a bottle of champagne and some dessert.

"You were wonderful tonight, my Jesse."

"Thank you. So were you. I was so proud to have you with me."

"I wouldn't have been anywhere else."

"Except maybe when Constance was there."

"Oh, Jesse. Must we?"

"I'd like to know what your story with her is."

Odette sank back in her chair.

"If you must know, she thinks I broke her heart. Which is nonsense."

"What happened?"

"She was here for a few weeks. We met. We got along. She claims she fell in love. I didn't."

"She was only here for a few weeks? What did she expect?"

"She wanted me to move home with her. It was crazy."

"What about us, Odette?"

"What about us?"

"Do you love me?"

"I do. This is different."

Jesse wanted to ask what was going to happen when her time in Paris was up, but opted against it. She wasn't sure she wanted to know the answer. She wasn't sure she knew what she wanted and was pretty sure she wasn't ready to hear what Odette wanted.

They sipped their champagne and shared their dessert. The silence was tense for Jesse, but Odette seemed to want to try to alleviate it.

"So, you did really well tonight, didn't you?" she asked.

"I did. It was a lot of fun. And now I have some money so I can take you out once in a while."

"True. It'll add to your allowance for sure."

"Yep."

"And it had to feel good. I'm sure you won't be that nervous next time."

"It felt really good. It was nice to get some sales under my belt. I'm sure the next one will be easier."

"Good, baby. That's very good to hear. When is the next student show?"

"In three months."

"That's not much time to paint a new set of paintings."

"It'll be enough. And think how much more I'll learn by then."

"True."

The silence that followed was deafening.

"Jesse, please. Why are you upset still?"

"I'm sorry. I'm trying not to be."

"We should be happy. Celebrating. Not worrying about something that happened years ago."

"How many years?"

"Oh, Jesse. I don't know. Five? Maybe six?"

"Really?"

"Yes. So I ask you. Are you jealous?"

"No. Yes. A little. I don't know."

"Why? It was before us. Why be jealous? And you never told me about your relationship with her. Did you ever have one?"

"A relationship?" Jesse thought how best to answer the question. "Our relationship has always been about me and my art."

"So you never slept with her?"

"Yes, I did."

"See? I'm not jealous."

"I know. I'm sorry. I'm being ridiculous."

"Relax, Jesse. You've been so tense these past few days. Allow yourself to relax and enjoy now that it's over."

"You're right. I'm sorry, Odette."

"It's okay. Now, where's my Jesse?"

Jesse gave her a big smile and took her hand. She resolved not to worry about Odette and Constance any more.

"So what will you be painting next?" Odette asked.

"I don't know. I'd like to do more cityscapes."

"Ah, yes. You captured Paris so well in some of those paintings."

"Really? Coming from you that means so much to me."

"You do good work, my Jesse. You need to believe me."

"Thank you. I do."

"I need to show you more of Paris. More for you to paint."

"That would be great."

"We'll do that. I'll take time off work."

"Can you do that?"

"Oh, Jesse. It'll be good for me to work less. I'd like to spend my weekends with you, if that's okay."

"That would be great." Jesse was excited at the prospect of more time with Odette. She couldn't get enough of her and spending every Saturday and Sunday with her sounded amazing to her.

"Good. I wanted to talk to you before I made my decision."

"Babe, I'd love to spend any time with you that you're available."

"Oh. I'm so excited. I need more time with you, Jesse. I don't get enough. We need to be together more."

"We do. I agree. I was so happy you were able to take this whole weekend off. I never dreamed you'd be able to do that every weekend."

"Well, I will. We'll have so much more time. And if you want, we can start spending nights at my house once in a while."

"That would be wonderful."

"For now, though, we should get back to your apartment. I want to keep celebrating."

"That sounds wonderful."

They walked through the streets, arm in arm. Jesse had forgotten Constance and was focusing only on her time with Odette.

They reached her apartment and fell into each other's arms. Nothing made Jesse forget the world like holding Odette. They made it to the bedroom and quickly undressed, then fell into bed together.

Jesse loved Odette slowly and completely. She started kissing her and worked her way down her body, leaving no spot unkissed. She paused to suck and nip at her breasts before kissing lower to her belly and below. She made herself at home between her legs and ran her tongue over everything she found. She reveled in her flavor and buried her tongue deep to taste all of her.

Odette squirmed on the bed, arching her back to encourage Jesse. Jesse continued to work until Odette cried out in her pleasure.

Jesse wasn't ready to stop. She moved her mouth to Odette's clit and sucked and licked it. Odette tried to protest, but Jesse wouldn't hear of it. She wasn't ready to stop. She needed more of Odette. She worked diligently and was rewarded as Odette called her name as she came.

Odette didn't rest long. She pulled Jesse to her and played her hands over her breasts.

"Your body is made for me to love, my Jesse."

She moved her hand between Jesse's legs and plunged her fingers deep inside her. Jesse moved against her, loving the feelings she was creating. She felt everything disappear except Odette's fingers and the sensations she experienced. She focused on Odette until she felt herself explode as the orgasm tore through her.

Jesse held Odette as they drifted off to sleep. The last thought she had was how wonderful it was that they had the next day together, as well.

CHAPTER NINETEEN

The next day, Odette surprised Jesse with a new digital camera so she could take pictures of everything she wanted to paint later. Jesse was thrilled and took Odette back to bed to thank her.

After their showers, Odette took Jesse to a neighborhood she had yet to explore. It was located closer to the center of town and the business district. But it was filled with trendy boutiques and they watched the shoppers mill about.

Jesse was again taken in by the bustling activity. She took picture after picture, determined to capture the essence of the neighborhood. She couldn't wait to paint this new place.

"Thank you so much for bringing me here," she said.

"I knew you'd like it. I want to do this on our Sundays together. Explore new areas."

"I love it. Thanks. And I love knowing we'll always have Sundays together."

"Yes, we will. Now how about lunch?"

"My treat."

They found a restaurant and settled in to eat and do more people watching. Jesse found herself falling more in love with Paris. She loved the people, the culture, the language. Though she couldn't speak a word of French, she loved listening to the lilting accents of those around her.

"This city is amazing," she said.

"I'm so glad you love it as I do."

"I really do. It's just so alive."

"It is. There is always something happening."

They spent their afternoon wandering through the boutiques and the rest of the neighborhood before heading home in the early evening.

Jesse made dinner for them. After, Odette read while Jesse sketched some of the scenes she had seen that day.

Odette looked up from her book.

"Jesse. You captured that so well. You are so talented."

"Thank you."

"I mean it. Your talent impresses me."

"I'm glad you think I'm talented. And I'm only going to get better with my instruction from the Academy."

"This is true. They make wonderful artists there."

"Yep. They'll mold me into the best artist I can be."

"And you'll become world famous."

Jesse laughed.

"You think so, huh?"

"I know so."

"I love the faith you have in me."

"I have so much. And you deserve it."

When Jesse finished sketching, they went to bed and made love late into the night. The next morning, they did it all again until Odette protested that she had to get to work.

Jesse was excited to get to school to find out how the show had done. Her instructors proclaimed it a success and told them how many art dealers had been there. Including the German man who'd bought Jesse's seascape. Jesse was thrilled to know her art was desirable to someone who really knew what good art was.

She focused harder on everything her teachers said and worked on improving her strokes and color combinations. She took everything to heart and tried new techniques to better her craft. She was determined to do right by Constance and make a name for herself in the art world.

The week flew by and Friday night rolled around. Jesse and Odette were both exhausted from their weeks. They opted for a quiet night at Odette's house. Madeline was home and the three of them ate dinner together and visited. It was a lovely evening and when it was time for bed, Jesse couldn't wait to get her hands on Odette.

"You're just so sexy. It kills me not to be able to devour you every minute of every day."

"Oh, my sweet Jesse, I love how you see me."

"I see you how you are, Odette. A gorgeous, sexy, vibrant woman who I can't get enough of."

"Come here, Jesse. Make love to me."

Jesse was happy to oblige. She loved her completely and when both women were spent, she held Odette close as they drifted off to sleep.

Jesse woke the next morning and rolled over to love Odette. She sucked her nipples and ran her hand between her legs. She found it odd that Odette didn't respond. She kissed her neck and face and still there was no reaction from Odette.

"Odette! Odette. Wake up."

Nothing.

"Madeline! Call nine one one!" She screamed down the hall.

Madeline came running.

"What?"

"Call nine one one."

"I don't understand."

"Odette's not waking up. Call an ambulance!"

Madeline called while Jesse stayed with Odette, begging her to wake up.

The ambulance arrived and Jesse rode to the hospital with Odette, who was still unconscious. Madeline followed in her car.

The paramedics did all they could to help Odette regain consciousness, but nothing was working. Jesse had a knot in her stomach. She was terrified. At least she's alive, she told herself. This wasn't Sara all over again.

They got to the emergency room and Jesse sat in a chair with Madeline in the room while the doctors examined Odette. They took her for an MRI and Jesse and Madeline were left alone.

"I'm scared," Madeline said.

Jesse hugged her, as much to reassure herself as Madeline. She was scared, too, and didn't know what to say to ease either of their minds.

They wheeled Odette back into the cubicle and the doctors spoke to Madeline in French. She started crying and turned to Jesse, who held her again, confused and more scared than ever.

"What did they say?"

Madeline just cried. Jesse turned to the doctor.

"In English, please. I don't speak French."

"Your friend has had a stroke."

The words hit her like a punch in the gut.

"What does that mean? I mean, I know what that means, but how bad is it? When will she come around?"

"We don't have answers right now. It was a substantial stroke. We'll just have to wait and see. We'll get her moved to the critical care unit so she can be observed around the clock."

Jesse appreciated them using American terms for her. But the reality of it didn't change. Odette's life was hanging by a thread and she was terrified. Part of her wanted to stay with Odette every second of every day, but part of her wanted to run away. She'd lost one partner already. She didn't know if she could stand to lose another. But she knew she couldn't do that. She'd stay with Odette no matter what.

Madeline and Jesse worked out a schedule so that one of them was with Odette at all times. Occasionally, they were both there, which helped Jesse since she couldn't understand anything the nurses said. A few of them could speak broken English, but for the most part, she was lost. Odette was still unconscious and that was all that mattered anyway.

Jesse managed to attend a few of her classes over the next several weeks, but she had explained to her professors what had happened. She did her homework for the ones she could and tried to make as many of the actual technique classes as was possible. Every moment she could spend with Odette, she did.

One Saturday morning, both Madeline and Jesse were sitting with Odette. Jesse was holding her hand, begging her to wake up, as was the norm.

Odette's eyes fluttered. They called a nurse, who came in, but Odette was still again. The nurse opened Odette's eyes and shined a light in them.

"She is more responsive," she said.

Odette opened her eyes on her own. She looked around and when her gaze fell on Jesse, she looked confused. She pulled her hand away.

"*Qui etes vou?*" she said.

Jesse looked at Madeline.

"What did she say? What does that mean?"

Odette looked at Madeline.

"*Qui est-ce?*"

"What is she saying?" Jesse was panicking. "Why isn't she speaking English?"

Madeline looked away from Jesse and Jesse could see her wiping a tear.

"What? What's going on?"

"She's asking who you are," Madeline said.

"What?"

"She doesn't know you, Jesse. I'm sorry. I'm so sorry."

"How could she not know me?"

"The doctor mentioned she might have short-term memory loss, Jesse."

"Yeah, but still..." She turned to Odette. "You really don't remember me?"

"*Je ne comprends pas.*"

"She doesn't understand you, Jesse."

"She doesn't understand English? She doesn't know who I am?" Jesse wanted to scream. How could this be happening?

The nurse was back with a doctor, who looked at Jesse.

"I think you should leave. I think you're upsetting her."

Jesse felt numb all over, but she did as she was asked. She caught a train back to her apartment and sunk into her couch. She buried her head in her hands and tried to comprehend that Odette had no recollection of her or their time together. She wondered if her memory would ever come back. She wanted to be there, to convince Odette that they loved each other and were a couple, but how could she do that if Odette didn't even understand English anymore?

She walked to her room and fell onto her bed. She tried to focus on something, anything but the horrible truth that faced her. But, she was surrounded by Odette. Her clothes were in her closet; her scent filled the air. She got up and left the apartment to go for a walk to clear her head.

She wandered down to the open-air market, hoping the vibrancy of it would help her mood. She bought a few things, but nothing was making her feel better. Then, she saw Amelie.

"Hello, Jesse! Where is your lovely lady friend?"

Jesse wasn't sure what to say; how to explain to Amelie what had happened.

"She's actually in the hospital," she said.

"Oh, no. I hope she'll be okay. Would you like to take her some flowers?"

"Not right now," Jesse said. She was feeling worse by the minute and just wanted to get away. "I'll talk to you later."

She took her purchases home and thought about making dinner, but she didn't have an appetite. She considered sketching, but had no desire to do that. She had no urge to do anything. She didn't want to go on living if it meant living without Odette, but she knew she had to. She just had to get through the next day and then she'd throw herself into her studies.

She checked her watch and saw that it would be a reasonable time to call Liza. That would do her good. She dialed the phone and was grateful that Liza picked up.

"Hey, stranger," Liza said. "How's my domesticated friend?"

"Not good."

"What's up?"

It was then that Jesse finally lost it. She began to sob uncontrollably.

"Jesse, hon, what's wrong?"

"She doesn't remember me."

"What? Who? What are you talking about?"

Jesse realized she'd been so busy keeping vigil that she'd never told Liza about Odette.

"Odette had a stroke. She was out of it for three weeks. She woke up today and doesn't know who I am."

"Oh, Jesse. I'm so sorry. What are you going to do?"

"What can I do?"

"I don't know. You could come home," Liza said.

Jesse was silent as the words sunk in. It was an option, to be sure. She could leave Paris and all the memories and pain behind and just go back to life as she knew it.

"Jess?"

"I'm here. Just thinking about what you said."

"How long do they think she'll be like that? Not knowing you, I mean."

"They don't know. It could be permanent."

"That's not good. How much longer are you there?"

"A long time."

"Come home, Jess."

"What would I do? I'd have to find a new job at my age. That wouldn't be good."

"Maybe that art lady could find some shows for you to do."

"The art lady? Oh, Constance? I doubt it. She wouldn't be happy if I quit the Academy."

"I'm sorry you're going through this. I wish I could take you out right now and get you drunk."

"Maybe that's what I should do. Go out and get drunk," Jesse said.

"Go for it. Just don't call me in the middle of *my* night all drunk, okay?"

"I have a few hours before that happens."

"Yes, you do. It's just noon here."

"Thanks for listening to me, Liza."

"Any time, Jess. I'm really sorry you're going through this."

"Me, too."

They said their good-byes and Jesse wandered out into the evening. She found a bar that catered mostly to the students from the Academy and walked in. She saw some familiar faces, but didn't join anyone. She needed to be alone.

She made her way to the bar and considered her order. She wanted something stronger than beer. She ordered a bourbon and water. She quickly finished it and ordered another. Then another. She was on her fourth one when a group of students invited her to join them and she did. She was buzzed enough not to care.

The group was lively and while she didn't fit in, she wasn't having a horrible time. She was on her fifth drink when her phone rang. She looked down and saw it was Madeline. Her heart skipped a beat. Maybe Odette was back. She excused herself and stepped outside to take the call.

"How is she?" Jesse asked.

"The same."

Jesse's heart sank.

"That sucks."

"Yes. It does. I'm sorry Jesse. I just wanted to tell you how sorry I am."

"Is she at least speaking English?"

"No. She pretty much went back to sleep after you left. She's woken up a few times, but she mostly sleeps."

"When will you get to take her home?"

"We don't know yet. It depends how bad the, um, damage is. She talks, which is good, but they haven't try to make her walk yet. She can grab with her hands, though, which is also good."

"I'm glad," Jesse said. She meant it. She was happy to hear Odette was going to be okay, if it turned out that way. But it still killed her inside that she could be fine in so many ways and not mentally.

The silence that followed was uncomfortable and Jesse finally broke it.

"Well, I guess I should let you go be with your mom."

"Yeah. I probably should."

"Keep me posted, Madeline, okay? She might not know who I am, but I'm not about to forget her."

"Will do, Jesse. Good-bye."

Jesse leaned against the outer wall of the bar and fought to keep the tears in check. She took some deep breaths, then went back in. She finished her drink and had one more, but was no longer in the mood to be there.

She walked back to her empty apartment feeling more alone than she had in years.

CHAPTER TWENTY

Jessie woke the next morning feeling horrible. Her head hurt, her stomach churned, and her heart ached. She tried to convince herself the day before had been a bad dream, but she knew better. She got up and thought about making coffee, but couldn't find the motivation. She decided to go to the café. Then she remembered again that Odette wouldn't be there.

Still, no Odette was better than an Odette who didn't know her, so she went across the street for some greasy food and coffee.

Giselle was at her table with a pot of coffee almost immediately.

"How is Odette?" She asked as she filled Jesse's cup.

"She woke up yesterday," Jesse said.

"She did? That's fantastic!"

"Yes. So far, it looks like she'll be okay."

"You don't seem too excited. And why are you here and not at the hospital?"

"She's not the same mentally," Jesse said.

"What do you mean?"

"Her memory is impaired."

"I don't know that word."

"She can't remember things. She doesn't speak or understand English, for one."

"Oh no. That's not good. What else?"

Jesse choked back her tears.

"She has no idea who I am."

"I'm sorry, Jesse. That breaks my heart."

"Yeah," Jesse said. She took a deep breath. "I don't know if she knows she owns the café or not. She seemed to know Madeline, so that's a good thing."

"That's so brave of you to look for something good."

"It's not easy."

"I'm sure it's not."

A few more patrons came in, so Giselle handed Jesse a menu, squeezed her shoulder and promised to be back in just a minute to take her order.

Jesse ordered her breakfast and pondered what to do with her day. All she had left was her art, so she decided after breakfast to go to school and paint.

She took her camera with her and looked at all the photos she had taken to see if any inspired her, but all they did was depress her. She sat in a chair flipping through picture after picture remembering the fun she and Odette had had.

"You don't look too enthused," a voice said.

Jesse looked up to see one of her professors standing next to her.

"I'm sorry. I didn't hear you come in."

"It's okay. But why the long face? You should be filled with joy and happiness when you come to paint. What are you looking at?"

"Pictures I took with a friend."

"Your friend in the hospital?"

"Yep." She didn't want to go into it. "I don't think any of these pictures will work."

"Then don't use them. Go with what's in your heart. Your art should always reflect your heart. We've said that how many times?"

"Yes, sir. I know that. I will. I'll paint from my heart."

The result was a stormy seascape. She worked hard on the sky, making it dark and gloomy with only a hint of moonlight showing through. She used dark blues and greens blended to make the sea. She stood back and looked at it when she had the basics painted.

Her professor walked over to look at it.

"Oh, my. That's a dark heart, but what a gorgeous piece of work."

"Really?"

"Really. Your strokes are wonderful, your use of shadows amazing. This is very good, Jesse. I can't wait to see the finished product."

Jesse's heart swelled at the compliment. It felt good to know something was going right in her life. Although, she kind of thought the painting was a finished product, but she could see that she could add more to it. But the paint had to dry before she did and she'd been at it all day. It was time to go home.

She stopped by the corner market and bought some beer and tequila and headed home. She took a long, hot shower then opened a beer and the bottle of tequila. She took a swig of the tequila and a pull on her beer. The combination tasted good and she quickly drank more tequila before setting the bottle down and taking her beer into her front room.

She opened a sketch pad and sat down to let some of the pain out. First, she sketched the outline. It was easy to do as it was forever embedded in her memory. Next came her eyes. She knew the exact shape of them and colored them the perfect shade of green. Then it was time to draw her nose. Her nose was so cute and had such a definite shape. When it was time to draw her mouth, a tear slid from Jesse's eye. How many times had that mouth smiled at her, laughed with her, and kissed her? She could draw it with her eyes closed. She set her sketch pad down and went to get some more tequila. When she came back, the picture of Odette staring back at her took her breath away. All that was left was her hair. She quickly drew the spiky gray hair that was all Odette. The picture was spot-on. And it was hers. It would never be in a show or given away. It was hers forever.

It was getting late and Jesse had school the next day, so she finished her beer and put the tequila away. She climbed into bed alone and cried herself to sleep.

❖

Jesse threw herself into her work. She hung on the words of every professor, studying how to paint and sketch better. She wanted to be significantly better by the next show. Her professors were all impressed with her work. They encouraged her to push harder and improve her techniques. And she rose to the occasion. Things were improving and she was feeling better about life.

Until she went home at night to her empty apartment. Then, nothing mattered. Not her art, not anything. The only thing that mattered was that Odette wasn't with her. She drowned her sorrows and passed out alone every night.

The time passed and she kept in touch with Madeline. At first, she checked in weekly, then every couple of weeks to see how Odette was doing. The news never changed. She was fine physically, but her memory was compromised and might never come back.

One Saturday morning, Jesse went across the street to the café and was surprised to see Madeline and Odette there. The pain in her heart was physical as she looked at the woman who had once loved her so deeply. She didn't go to their table, but Madeline came over to see her.

"She looks great," Jesse said.

"She's doing very well. She's working on her English so she can come back to the café. She knows she owns it, but needs to speak English to work here. It's coming back quite easily for her. It's only a matter of time before she's back."

"Good for her. If only she could remember me."

"I'm sorry, Jesse. I wish she did as well."

"You'll keep me posted, right?"

"Of course, Jesse. I'll let you know if there's any change at all."

"Thank you."

Jesse finished her breakfast and went to school to paint. She painted with her heart and it was another stormy picture. That seemed to be all she could paint anymore. She finished all she could and touched up another picture she had in progress and then it was late and time for her to go home.

Jesse was determined to paint more than simply stormy seascapes for the next show that was rapidly approaching. So, she made a point every weekend of visiting new neighborhoods in the city and studying them to paint. She got back to painting cityscapes and they turned out very well, in her opinion. And in the opinion of several of her instructors. The general consensus was that her talent had significantly improved. She was pleased at the positive feedback and began to convince herself that her art was all she really needed anyway.

The second art show arrived and Jesse tried not to dwell on the first one where Odette was there to support her. She got everything set up the way she wanted and wandered about checking out the other exhibits. She had some talented classmates, to be sure, but knew her work was very good, too. She felt good about what she was doing and wasn't nearly as nervous for this show.

The guests finally showed up and she was happy to have so many people crowded around her exhibit. She sold several stormy seascapes and many of her cityscapes. The paintings seemed to be flying off their easels and at one point she could barely keep up with customers.

Things had slowed down a bit and Jesse was relaxing when Amelie walked up.

"Hello, Jesse."

"Amelie." Jesse stood and hugged her. "What brings you here?"

"I come to these once in a while. Just to see what students are up to. And since I knew you would be here, I wanted to see your work."

"Well, thank you for supporting us. I appreciate it."

"You don't have much on display."

"I've sold a lot of stuff this evening."

"Good for you. Where's your lady friend?"

Jesse's stomach clenched. She figured she might as well be honest.

"We're not together anymore."

"Oh, Jesse. I'm sorry."

"It's been a while, so it's okay. Thank you, though."

"What are you doing after the show tonight?"

"I hadn't really thought about it."

"We'll go out to celebrate. It'll be fun."

Jesse wasn't sure she was up for going out, but another night alone in her apartment didn't appeal to her, either.

"What time should I come back?" Amelie asked.

Jesse had to laugh. Clearly, she was going out.

"The show ends at ten."

"Perfect. We'll go get dinner then drink and dance. It'll be fun. Besides, you look like you need to get out."

"I probably do."

"Yes. You do. I'll see you at ten."

The rest of the evening passed more slowly for Jesse. She found herself getting nervous at the prospect of going out with Amelie. She didn't know why. She was a free woman and Amelie was an attractive woman who she'd had fun with before. She told herself to relax and have fun.

She was packing up her things when Amelie returned.

"Give me just a few minutes," Jesse said.

"I'm not going anywhere."

"Good." Jesse liked Amelie and was no longer tense about the night ahead.

She finished putting her things away, locked her locker unit, and walked back to Amelie.

"So, where are we going?"

"We will stay in the neighborhood tonight. There are plenty of places around here. I'm hungry, though, so we'll go to dinner now."

Jesse had to smile at Amelie's directness. She had forgotten how she liked to call the shots.

"Lead the way," she said.

They walked down the street to a small café. Jesse knew enough French by then to order on her own. They sipped wine and talked about the art show.

"You are very good, Jesse. I had no idea."

"Thank you."

"Of course, I should have guessed. You are a very passionate woman. I should have known you would be passionate about your art."

Jesse blushed, thinking of the passionate night they'd shared. "Thank you. I'm happy with how the show went."

"Good. I'm happy for you."

They ate their dinner and shared two bottles of wine. Jesse was feeling good by the time they left to go dancing. Amelie took them to a place a few doors down from the café. It was dimly lit with a good crowd and loud music.

Jesse ordered Amelie a champagne and herself a beer, and they found one of the few open tables and made themselves comfortable. As comfortable as Jesse could get, anyway, with Amelie sitting against her. She felt guilty and chided herself there was no reason to feel that way. She placed her arm around Amelie's shoulders and pulled her closer. She was single and so was Amelie. There was no reason not to make the most of their night.

Amelie stood abruptly.

"It's time to dance."

What could Jesse do? She followed her to the dance floor and watched her slim figure sway and twist in rhythm with the music. Amelie had a sexy body and Jesse couldn't take her eyes off her.

Jesse moved with ease as she watched Amelie. She let the music flow over her and relax her. Life was good. The art show was a success. Amelie was beautiful. And the night was ahead of them. What more could she ask for? She didn't dwell on that thought.

They danced several more fast songs before the music finally slowed. Amelie moved into Jesse's arms. Jesse held her loosely as they moved together. It felt good to feel Amelie moving against her, but she was careful not to pull her too close. Not yet. She wasn't quite ready for that.

When the song ended, Amelie pressed close to Jesse. Jesse's first instinct was to move away, but she stood her ground. Amelie simply hugged her. She took Jesse's hand and led her back to the table. Jesse was very aware of the soft warmth of Amelie's skin and knew she could feel so much more of it if she wanted.

They were seated at the table with Amelie against Jesse again.

"Are you okay?" Amelie asked.

"I'm great."

"Are you having fun?"

"I am."

"Good. You seem nervous."

"Not me," Jesse lied.

"I'm glad. I just want to have fun."

"Me, too."

"Then, kiss me, Jesse."

Jesse hesitated only briefly before kissing Amelie. It was a soft kiss, but Amelie demanded more. Jesse gave in and felt her body come alive. She pulled Amelie to her and got lost in the kiss.

The minute it ended, she was overcome with guilt.

"I'm sorry, Amelie. I can't…"

Amelie gazed into her eyes.

"You are not over her."

"No. I'm not."

"Tell me."

"What?"

"Come. We'll walk. You'll tell me about her."

They left the bar. The night air felt good and the space made it easier for Jesse to breathe.

"What happened?" Amelie asked.

"She had a stroke."

"A stroke?"

"Yes. It affects the brain."

"Oh. Okay."

"Anyway, she doesn't remember me."

"That is horrible."

"Yeah, it sucks."

Amelie took Jesse's hand.

"But you are a grown woman with needs. You should not feel guilty or deny yourself."

"I know that in my head."

"I'm not trying to replace her," Amelie said. "And I want nothing more than tonight."

"I get that. And I want you, Amelie. I just can't do this. I'm sorry."

"Do not be sorry. Your heart is not ready. And when it is, you know where to find me."

"Thank you, Amelie."

"You're welcome, Jesse."

She kissed Jesse's cheek and walked off into the night.

CHAPTER TWENTY-ONE

Autumn in Paris was beautiful. The light rain that fell seemed to cleanse the city after the summer heat. The way the sun hit the buildings and trees was so different and offered Jesse new colors and lightings to use in her paintings. It felt like a rebirth to her. And she welcomed it.

She worked late into the night on her paintings, doing her best to capture the new sense of life that emanated from the city she'd come to love. She worked with her colors to capture the play of sunlight through the mist in the early morning hours. She felt excited about how the paintings were coming and she'd always hate to leave school to go home.

One morning, after an extremely late night at school, she told herself it would be okay to go to the café to get some coffee and breakfast. She hadn't been in months as she hadn't been able to face Odette. She knew she might see her that morning and she steeled herself. She tried to tell herself enough time had passed and seeing Odette wouldn't be painful.

She saw her as soon as she entered the café. She was over at the counter pouring coffee. The pain was there, but it had lessened over time. She just hoped she wouldn't be sitting in her section. Having her wait on her as if she was a stranger would be too hard to handle.

Jesse sat in an open booth and cursed to herself when Odette walked over.

"Hi. What can I get for you?" she asked.

"I'll have the sausage and egg omelet and a cup of coffee."

"Coming right up."

Jesse watched her walk off, the familiar sway of her hips causing a stir deep inside her. It hurt her to know that Odette felt nothing for her.

Odette was back with her coffee.

"Thank you. I haven't seen you in a while," Jesse said.

"I was gone for a while. I own the place, so I'm back now."

"Oh. That's cool." Jesse was feeling sadder by the moment.

"I haven't seen you here before."

"I used to come in a lot."

"Really?"

"Yeah. I used to see you here. But then not for a while."

"Well, welcome back. My name's Odette."

"I'm Jesse."

Jesse thought she saw something change in Odette's eyes. She stared at her, wishing for a sure sign of recognition.

"Nice to meet you, Jesse."

She watched her walk off again and her heart sank. She lost her appetite, but made herself stay. She felt like a masochist, but she wanted more time with Odette. She still hoped against all hope that she'd remember her someday.

Odette brought her breakfast and smiled at her. It was a warm smile, not filled with the love that had once been so apparent on her face every time they saw each other, but it was a nice smile and Jesse smiled genuinely back at her.

"You seem familiar," Odette said.

Jesse's heart raced. She longed to tell Odette about them, but didn't know what kind of response she'd get. And she didn't want to scare Odette.

"You must remember me from when I used to come in."

"Maybe."

Jesse felt a glimmer of hope at the exchange. If she seemed familiar, there was a possibility it would all come back to her. At least, that's what she told herself. She finished her breakfast and went to school.

She was distracted in class, but when it came time to paint, her heart sang. She painted a castle under a bright blue sky. It was unusual for her, but she felt like her fairy tale ending might come true finally. She tried to caution herself, but her happiness was uncontainable. She used bold strokes and made the sun shine brightly on the ramparts.

One of her professors walked up and looked over her shoulder.

"That's fantastic, Jesse. You're doing great work. You've come a long way."

Jesse smiled.

"Thank you. It feels good."

"You're a natural. And it shows."

"I'm so glad. I've certainly learned a lot over the past few months."

"Good. You've been working hard and that's the key to success."

"I'll continue to work hard. I want to be the best I can be."

"That's the attitude we like, Jesse. Keep up the good work."

Jesse felt light as she finished as much of her painting as she could. She put her supplies away and walked home. Her phone rang just as she got home. It was Madeline. They hadn't talked in forever. Jesse was immediately afraid that something had happened to Odette.

"Hello?"

"Hey, Jesse. It's Madeline."

"Hey. What's up? Is everything okay?"

"Yeah. *Maman* just got home. She said she saw you today."

"She did? And?"

"She said you seemed very familiar to her."

"Yeah. She told me that at the café. Did she say anything else?"

"No, but I wanted you to know. I think that's a good sign, don't you?"

"I hope so, Madeline. It gives me a little hope anyway. Did you tell her about us?"

"No. I didn't know if I should. I'm sorry."

"It's okay. I don't know if you should, either."

"How are you doing, Jesse? I mean, really."

"I'm doing well. I'm throwing myself into my art, which is a good thing. But I miss her, you know? I still miss her."

"I'm sure you do. I wish she'd remember you, too. You made her so happy."

"She made me very happy, too."

"I know."

The silence that followed was awkward and Jesse finally ended it.

"I should probably let you go," she said.

"Yeah. I should get back to her."

"Thank you for calling, Madeline."

"You're welcome, Jesse. You take care of yourself."

They said their good-byes and Jesse sat on her couch. It had been several months since Odette's stroke. She should have moved on by now. But she couldn't. She held on to the hope that someday they would be back together. In some ways this was harder than losing Sara. At least when Sara went, she was gone. And in reality, Odette was gone, too, but there was a sliver of hope that she would be back. And that sliver is what Jesse held on to.

The next morning, Jesse woke late so didn't have time to stop at the café for breakfast. She really wanted to see Odette again, believing that the more she saw her, the more likely it was to jog her memory. She had no idea if that was truly the case, but she convinced herself it was worth a try.

She made it through her classes, but rather than stay late to paint, she hurried to the café for dinner. The place was packed and she had to wait for a table, but it was worth it as she ended up in Odette's section again.

"Jesse," Odette said. "It's nice to see you again."

"Nice to see you, too."

Jesse wondered if she should flirt with Odette. She thought since she'd found her attractive before, maybe she'd like her again. But she didn't want a new relationship with Odette. She wanted their old one back.

"It is busy tonight, but can I start you with a drink?"

Jesse ordered her beer and sat back to look at the menu. It was hard to act like she didn't have the whole thing memorized. When Odette came back, Jesse ordered the special and sat back to enjoy her beer.

She watched Odette move effortlessly among the tables, taking orders and bringing food. She wanted her to come sit with her like she used to, but even with as busy as it was, she wouldn't have been able to anyway.

Odette brought her food and stopped for just a moment.

"I feel like I know you."

"You did."

"You seem like a nice person. Maybe that's why I remember you."

Every bone in Jesse's body wanted her to scream out that they had once loved each other; that they were meant to be together, but she held her tongue.

"That could be it."

"I'll work on my brain. Sometimes things come back to me. I feel like I should remember you."

"You do that. If you remember me, that would be great."

Jesse ate her dinner and paid. She was out the front door when she heard Odette call her name.

"Jesse!"

Jesse turned and saw Odette coming toward her, arms wide.

"Oh, my Jesse! I remember you!"

Jesse opened her arms and pulled her into a powerful embrace. They stood like that for what seemed like forever. Jesse never wanted to let go, but Odette finally pulled away. She put her hands on either side of Jesse's face.

"Oh, my Jesse. It's been months. I can't believe I didn't remember you."

"It was hard, Odette. It's been so hard."

"Am I too late, Jesse? Have you found someone else?"

"No, Odette. I've been waiting for you. It hasn't been easy, but I've waited, hoping you'd get your memory back someday."

"I knew there was something about you when you were here yesterday. It bothered me all day and today, as well. I couldn't stop trying to figure out how I knew you."

"I was so hoping seeing me again might jog your memory."

"What if it didn't Jesse? Oh, what if I'd never remembered you again?"

"It's okay. We never have to worry about that."

"I need to get back to work. May I come over after work?"

"I'd like that."

"Do I still have clothes there?"

"No. Madeline took them all home."

"Well, I have some spare clothes here, in case I spill. I'll bring something with me to wear tomorrow." She paused. "That is, assuming you'd like me to stay the night?"

"I'd love nothing more, Odette."

"Good. I'll get back to it, then. I'll see you in a few hours. You'll have to come get me, though. I must admit I don't remember where you live."

Jesse's step was light as she walked home. She couldn't wipe the smile off her face. The first thing she did was call Madeline.

"Hello?"

"Madeline, it's Jesse."

"Hi, Jesse. Is everything okay?"

"Everything is great! I just wanted to let you know your mom won't be coming home tonight."

"No?" There was a pause. "No? She won't, huh? Will she be staying with you?"

"Yes, she will. She remembers me and is coming over after work."

"Jesse! That's fantastic news. I'm so happy for you."

"Thanks, Madeline. I wanted you to be the first to know."

"That's great. Take good care of her. She's still not quite right. But this is a huge step."

"I will. And you're right. This is a giant step."

They said their good-byes, and Jesse wondered what to do for the next couple of hours.

She took a shower and opened a bottle of wine. Then she opened her sketch pad and began to sketch to kill the time.

Jesse checked her watch every few minutes and was happy when it was just past ten. She walked back to the café just as Odette was stepping outside.

They walked to Jesse's apartment.

"Does any of this look familiar?" Jesse asked.

"A little."

"I'm glad you're getting your memory back."

"Me, too. I'm so happy I remembered you."

"I hope the rest of it comes back soon."

"So do I."

They arrived at the apartment and Jesse poured them each a glass of wine.

"Do you still like wine?" she asked.

"I do."

"Good. I need to remember that things might have changed."

"I'm pretty much back to normal, I think," Odette said.

"That's good to hear."

Odette wandered into the front room and looked around.

"This is all very familiar to me."

"That's a very good sign."

Odette turned to Jesse.

"Thank you so much for waiting for me."

"How could I not?"

"You didn't have to, Jesse. And I know that. It must have been frustrating."

"It was horrible at first. Then I threw myself into my art and that eased the pain a little."

"I'm so sorry I put you through that, Jesse."

"It's okay. You're back now. That's all that matters."

"Jesse?"

"What?"

"Are you sure you feel the same way? I mean, nothing's changed for you?"

"I'm sure. Why?"

"Will you please kiss me then?"

"Are you sure you're ready?"

"I'm more than ready."

Jesse leaned in slowly until her lips barely brushed against Odette's. The shockwaves coursed through her system at the slight touch, and she knew she needed more. She placed her hand behind Odette's head and pulled her closer, pressing her tongue against her lips. Odette opened her mouth, and Jesse slid her tongue inside.

Their tongues danced together as their bodies moved closer. Soon they were pressed together and the heat from Odette's body was giving Jesse shivers.

"I need you, Odette."

"Take me, Jesse. It's been too long. Take me and make me yours."

They walked into the bedroom, where they kissed some more and Jesse began to undress Odette.

"I love you, Jesse. I still love you so very much."

"I love you, too, Odette. I have never stopped loving you."

Odette stood naked before Jesse and Jesse couldn't take her gaze away from the beautiful body in front of her.

"You are magnificent, Odette," she whispered.

"Please, Jesse," Odette said. "Please take your clothes off. I want to see you."

Jesse complied and soon stood naked with Odette. She pulled her against her and felt her own temperature rise as skin touched skin. They kissed passionately and rubbed against each other, Jesse lost in the sensations of holding Odette again.

Jesse eased Odette onto the bed and lay next to her.

"Are you okay?" she asked.

"Never better, my love."

Jesse skimmed her hand over Odette's body, taking in the silky feel of her skin.

"I've missed you so, Odette."

"I am so sorry, Jesse."

"Hush. It's okay. We're here now."

Jesse kissed her again as her hand moved to slide over a hard nipple. She ran her palm over it, feeling it poking her. She caressed the whole breast then, feeling how soft and supple it was. The feelings were driving her mad with passion. She cautioned herself to take things slowly. She wasn't completely convinced Odette would be okay.

"Jesse." Odette seemed to read her mind. "I was hurt mentally, not physically. Please do not be afraid."

"I'm just taking my time. I want to savor this, babe."

"Promise me you're not afraid. Because I am not. It has been too long, my Jesse."

Odette took Jesse's hand and placed it between her legs.

"Feel me Jesse. I'm ready for you."

Jesse's breath caught at how warm and wet Odette was. She moved her hand all over her, feeling her slick, hard clit before slipping inside her.

"Oh my God, you feel amazing," she said.

"Oh, so do you," Odette said. "Please. More. Don't stop."

"I'm not about to stop."

Jesse bent to take a nipple in her mouth as she continued to plunge deep inside Odette. She rubbed her palm on Odette's clit as she entered her and soon Odette was writhing on the bed, moving beneath Jesse in a frantic manner.

Jesse drew hard on the nipple and plunged as deep as she could, holding her hand in place as Odette screamed out her name and came again and again.

When Odette was silent, Jesse started again, this time moving inside her for a short period before moving her fingers to her swollen clit. She pinched her clit between her fingers before pressing into it and rubbing circles.

In no time, Odette was crying out again. Jesse glowed at being able to provide such pleasure to her, but she was a horny mess by that time.

Jesse climbed up next to Odette and took her in her arms.

"You are amazing, Odette."

"No. It is you who is amazing. And now I get to show you how much I love you."

She kissed Jesse on her mouth, her neck, and her shoulder.

"You taste amazing, my love."

She kissed down to take a nipple in her mouth and swirl her tongue around it. Jesse felt the electricity shoot to her clit. She didn't know how much she'd be able to take before begging Odette to touch her. She needn't have worried.

Odette released the nipple and Jesse felt the cool night air blow over it. Odette kissed down her belly, stopping to tease her belly button. She kissed lower still and settled between Jesse's legs.

"Oh, Jesse. How is it I've been without this all these months?"

"It's been a long time," Jesse managed, her whole body a bundle of knots needing release.

"You are beautiful," Odette said. She spread Jesse's lips and examined them. Jesse felt every touch in her very core.

Finally, Odette bent to taste her. Jesse felt her tongue on her clit and in her center. She spread her legs wider and begged silently for the climax to arrive. Odette hadn't forgotten how to please her. That was obvious as Jesse felt the knots come undone and the powerful orgasm wash over her.

Odette moved next to Jesse who embraced her with all the love she was feeling.

"I love you so much, Odette."

"I love you, too, my Jesse."

Jesse drifted off to sleep happy to have Odette in her arms instead of just her dreams.

About the Author

MJ Williamz is the author of over thirty short stories, mostly erotica with a few romance and horrors thrown in for good measure. She is also the author of eight novels, including two Goldie winners—*Initiation by Desire* and *Escapades*. She lives in Houston with her wife and son.

Visit MJ's website at www.mjwilliamz.com, friend her on Facebook, or follow her on Twitter: @mj_williamz.

Books Available from Bold Strokes Books

A Reunion to Remember by TJ Thomas. Reunited after a decade, Jo Adams and Rhonda Black must navigate a significant age difference, family dynamics, and their own desires and fears to explore an opportunity for love. (978-1-62639-534-3)

Built to Last by Aurora Rey. When Professor Olivia Bennett hires contractor Joss Bauer to restore her dilapidated farmhouse, she learns her heart, as much as her house, is in need of a renovation. (978-1-62639-552-7)

Capsized by Julie Cannon. What happens when a woman turns your life completely upside down? (978-1-62639-479-7)

Girls With Guns by Ali Vali, Carsen Taite, and Michelle Grubb. Three stories by three talented crime writers—Carsen Taite, Ali Vali, and Michelle Grubb—each packing her own special brand of heat. (978-1-62639-585-5)

Heartscapes by MJ Williamz. Will Odette ever recover her memory or is Jesse condemned to remember their love alone? (978-1-62639-532-9)

Murder on the Rocks by Clara Nipper. Detective Jill Rogers lives with two things on her mind: sex and murder. While an ice storm cripples Tulsa, two things stand in Jill's way: her lover and the DA. (978-1-62639-600-5)

Necromantia by Sheri Lewis Wohl. When seeing dead people is more than a movie tagline. (978-1-62639-611-1)

Salvation by I. Beacham. Claire's long-term partner now hates her, for all the wrong reasons, and she sees no future until she meets

Regan, who challenges her to face the truth and find love. (978-1-62639-548-0)

Trigger by Jessica Webb. Dr. Kate Morrison races to discover how to defuse human bombs while learning to trust her increasingly strong feelings for the lead investigator, Sergeant Andy Wyles. (978-1-62639-669-2)

24/7 by Yolanda Wallace. When the trip of a lifetime becomes a pitched battle between life and death, will anyone survive? (978-1-62639-6-197)

A Return to Arms by Sheree Greer. When a police shooting makes national headlines, activists Folami and Toya struggle to balance their relationship and political allegiances, a struggle intensified after a fiery young artist enters their lives. (978-1-62639-6-814)

After the Fire by Emily Smith. Paramedic Connor Haus is convinced her time for love has come and gone, but when firefighter Logan Curtis comes into town, she learns it may not be too late after all. (978-1-62639-6-524)

Dian's Ghost by Justine Saracen. The road to genocide is paved with good intentions. (978-1-62639-5-947)

Fortunate Sum by M. Ullrich. Financial advisor Catherine Carter lives a calculated life, but after a collision with spunky Imogene Harris (her latest client) and unsolicited predictions, Catherine finds herself facing an unexpected variable: Love. (978-1-62639-5-305)

Soul to Keep by Rebekah Weatherspoon. What *won't* a vampire do for love... (978-1-62639-6-166)

When I Knew You by KE Payne. Eight letters, three friends, two lovers, one secret. Can the past ever be forgiven? (978-1-62639-5-626)

Wild Shores by Radclyffe. Can two women on opposite sides of an oil spill find a way to save both a wildlife sanctuary and their hearts? (978-1-62639-6-456)

Love on Tap by Karis Walsh. Beer and romance are brewing for Tace Lomond when archaeologist Berit Katsaros comes into her life. (987-1-162639-564-0)

Love on the Red Rocks by Lisa Moreau. An unexpected romance at a lesbian resort forces Malley to face her greatest fears where she must choose between playing it safe or taking a chance at true happiness. (987-1-162639-660-9)

Tracker and the Spy by D. Jackson Leigh. There are lessons for all when Captain Tanisha is assigned untried pyro Kyle and a lovesick dragon horse for a mission to track the leader of a dangerous cult. (987-1-162639-448-3)

Whirlwind Romance by Kris Bryant. Will chasing the girl break Tristan's heart or give her something she's never had before? (987-1-162639-581-7)

Whiskey Sunrise by Missouri Vaun. Culture and religion collide when Lovey Porter, daughter of a local Baptist minister, falls for the handsome thrill-seeking moonshine runner, Royal Duval. (987-1-162639-519-0)

Dyre: By Moon's Light by Rachel E. Bailey. A young werewolf, Des, guards the aging leader of all the Packs: the Dyre. Stable employment—nice work, if you can get it...at least until silver bullets start to fly. (978-1-62639-6-623)

Fragile Wings by Rebecca S. Buck. In Roaring Twenties London, can Evelyn Hopkins find love with Jos Singleton or will the scars of the Great War crush her dreams? (978-1-62639-5-466)

Live and Love Again by Jan Gayle. Jessica Whitney could be Sarah Jarret's second chance at love, but their differences and Sarah's grief continue to come between their budding relationship. (978-1-62639-5-176)

Starstruck by Lesley Davis. Actress Cassidy Hayes and writer Aiden Darrow find out the hard way not all life-threatening drama is confined to the TV screen or the pages of a manuscript. (978-1-62639-5-237)

Stealing Sunshine by Tina Michele. Under the Central Florida sun, two women struggle between fear and love as a dangerous plot of deception and revenge threatens to steal priceless art and lives. (978-1-62639-4-452)

The Fifth Gospel by Michelle Grubb. Hiding a Vatican secret is dangerous—sharing the secret suicidal—can Felicity survive a perilous book tour, and will her PR specialist, Anna, be there when it's all over? (978-1-62639-4-476)

Cold to the Touch by Cari Hunter. A drug addict's murder is the start of a dangerous investigation for Detective Sanne Jensen and Dr. Meg Fielding, as they try to stop a killer with no conscience. (978-1-62639-526-8)

Forsaken by Laydin Michaels. The hunt for a killer teaches one woman that she must overcome her fear in order to love, and another that success is meaningless without happiness. (978-1-62639-481-0)

Infiltration by Jackie D. When a CIA breach is imminent, a Marine instructor must stop the attack while protecting her heart from being disarmed by a recruit. (978-1-62639-521-3)

Midnight at the Orpheus by Alyssa Linn Palmer. Two women desperate to make their way in the world, a man hell-bent on revenge, and a cop risking his career: all in a day's work in Capone's Chicago. (978-1-62639-607-4)

Spirit of the Dance by Mardi Alexander. Major Sorla Reardon's return to her family farm to heal threatens Riley Johnson's safe life when small-town secrets are revealed, and love may not conquer all. (978-1-62639-583-1)

Sweet Hearts by Melissa Brayden, Rachel Spangler, and Karis Walsh. Do you ever wonder *Whatever happened to...*? Find out when you reconnect with your favorite characters from Melissa Brayden's *Heart Block*, Rachel Spangler's *LoveLife*, and Karis Walsh's *Worth the Risk*. (978-1-62639-475-9)

Totally Worth It by Maggie Cummings. Who knew there's an all-lesbian condo community in the NYC suburbs? Join twentysomething BFFs Meg and Lexi at Bay West as they navigate friendships, love, and everything in between. (978-1-62639-512-1)

Illicit Artifacts by Stevie Mikayne. Her foster mother's death cracked open a secret world Jil never wanted to see...and now she has to pick up the stolen pieces. (978-1-62639-472-8)

Pathfinder by Gun Brooke. Heading for their new homeworld, Exodus's chief engineer Adina Vantressa and nurse Briar Lindemay carry game-changing secrets that may well cause them to lose everything when disaster strikes. (978-1-62639-444-5)

Prescription for Love by Radclyffe. Dr. Flannery Rivers finds herself attracted to the new ER chief, city girl Abigail Remy, and the incendiary mix of city and country, fire and ice, tradition and change is combustible. (978-1-62639-570-1)

Ready or Not by Melissa Brayden. Uptight Mallory Spencer finds relinquishing control to bartender Hope Sanders too tall an order in fast-paced New York City. (978-1-62639-443-8)

Summer Passion by MJ Williamz. Women loving women is forbidden in 1946 Hollywood, yet Jean and Maggie strive to keep their love alive and away from prying eyes. (978-1-62639-540-4)

The Princess and the Prix by Nell Stark. "Ugly duckling" Princess Alix of Monaco was resigned to loneliness until she met racecar driver Thalia d'Angelis. (978-1-62639-474-2)

Winter's Harbor by Aurora Rey. Lia Brooks isn't looking for love in Provincetown, but when she discovers chocolate croissants and pastry chef Alex McKinnon, her winter retreat quickly starts heating up. (978-1-62639-498-8)

The Time Before Now by Missouri Vaun. Vivian flees a disastrous affair, embarking on an epic, transformative journey to escape her past, until destiny introduces her to Ida, who helps her rediscover trust, love, and hope. (978-1-62639-446-9)